"According to Charlie, my name means 'beloved,'" Roxie said.

The back of her neck grew warm. She knew Hank was staring at her, and she was afraid to turn around and catch him at it.

"It seems a strange coincidence that according to Charlie, *my* last name means 'abounding in love,'" Hank commented.

"Yes, but I'm sure it's only a coincidence." By now she knew it wasn't. Where Hank was concerned, she had no control over her feelings...or her desires.

"'Beloved,'" Hank repeated. "That sounds good. It suits you, Roxie. Tell me, what does Charlie think will happen if two people with names like ours meet on St. Valentine's Day?"

She glanced up at him. "Oh, as you can imagine, he thinks we're destined for each other." She tried to laugh, as if it was a joke, but the laugh stuck in her throat.

"Do you think we are?" Hank asked as he wrapped his arms around Roxie's waist. "Because Charlie or no Charlie, I *am* going to love you, my *beloved*...."

Vicki Lewis Thompson began her writing career at the age of eleven with a short story in the *Auburn Illinois Weekly* and quickly became a byline junkie. Then she discovered she could write books—and she's written a lot of them! In the year 2000, Vicki saw her 50th book on the shelves. Vicki lives in Tucson, Arizona, and has two grown children and a husband who encourages her to write from the heart.

For Lisa,
who loves old movies and taking chances
(among other things)

ISBN 0-373-63181-2

BE MINE, VALENTINE

Copyright © 1989 by Vicki Lewis Thompson.

Visit us at www.eHarlequin.com

Printed in U.S.A.

VICKI LEWIS THOMPSON

Be Mine, Valentine

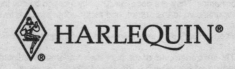

HARLEQUIN®

TORONTO • NEW YORK • LONDON
AMSTERDAM • PARIS • SYDNEY • HAMBURG
STOCKHOLM • ATHENS • TOKYO • MILAN • MADRID
PRAGUE • WARSAW • BUDAPEST • AUCKLAND

It began with the snow. Years later Roxie would wonder if old Charlie had arranged that, too. After all, if he'd told the truth about himself, then creating a little snowstorm in February wouldn't have taken much effort, even in the middle of the desert. The unusual weather could have been a coincidence, of course. Everything that happened afterward could have been a coincidence.

ON THAT FRIDAY AFTERNOON when the snow hit Tucson, Roxie couldn't believe the fuss over a few drifting flakes. After twenty-seven winters in New Jersey she'd seen enough white stuff to last her forever. Apparently that wasn't true of her co-workers in the county clerk's office. With the first incredulous cry of "It's snowing!" a few rushed to the windows and the rest hurried outside to catch the snow on hands and tongues.

Like children, Roxie thought. People who had patiently held numbers awaiting a turn at the counter left, too, until the office was nearly deserted. Roxie couldn't imagine more excitement if there'd been a ticker-tape parade for the president. Well, she'd seen snow before and she'd stay at her desk and finish up whatever work she could before quitting time. Because of her choice she was the only one who noticed when old Charlie trudged into the waiting area, his battered briefcase in his hand as always.

"What a pleasant surprise, Charlie." Roxie left her typewriter and went up to the counter for a little chat. Snow wasn't interesting enough to leave her work for, but Charlie was. She considered him her best friend in Tucson, which wasn't saying much for her social life in the past six months, she thought ruefully. Charlie was a sweet old man, but everyone in the office acknowledged that he was a bum.

His home was a bench in a nearby park and his closet was the old briefcase he carried everywhere. He ate wherever free meals were offered within walking distance of the park. He had some source of income, however, because every weekday morning he brought a single red rose into the county clerk's office and placed it in the bud vase on the gray laminated counter. He said the gesture was in honor of the couples who applied for marriage licenses there.

In return someone in the office usually provided his lunch. Lately, since she'd gotten promoted to the regular day shift, that someone had been Roxie. Packing two sandwiches wasn't much more trouble than packing one, and besides, she liked Charlie's company.

"So what brings you here this afternoon?" Roxie leaned against the counter and smiled at Charlie.

"Those lovely blue-green eyes and red curls, my dear. What else?"

"Come on, Charlie. My lovely eyes and red curls never dragged you away from your afternoon game of chess before. What gives?"

Charlie winked at her. "Actually the weather has altered and become a bit nasty, so I decided to take refuge in the temperate climate of your office." Charlie took off his worn fedora and brushed moisture from the scraggly feather stuck in the hatband. "When I chose to winter in Arizona, who would have imagined that I'd encounter snow?"

Roxie always got a kick out of listening to Charlie, who

sounded like a genteel professor from some European university. From a distance he even looked the part with his briefcase and a folded copy of the morning paper, but a closer view revealed the ragged sleeve of his tweed sport coat, a missing button on his vest, a torn pocket on his slacks, and rubbed-through edges on his red bow tie.

Employees began filtering back into the clerk's office. "It's sticking!" someone announced gleefully. "I think we should go home early, in case the roads get bad."

Roxie shook her head. "I've never seen such nonsense over a little snow."

"It's the intoxication of the unexpected," Charlie said.

"That's a good assessment. I suppose you're right." Roxie speculated for the hundredth time how a seemingly well-educated man ended up on the streets. "I don't want to embarrass you or anything, but...what will you do if it gets really cold tonight?"

Charlie gave her a piercing yet pleased glance, as if she were his star pupil and she'd just asked the right question. "I haven't the slightest idea," he said, taking out a surprisingly snowy handkerchief to polish the figure-eight-shaped pin he always wore on his lapel.

Roxie had decided weeks ago that the pin was indeed real gold. The pin and the pewter chess set he carried in his briefcase were probably the only things of value Charlie possessed. He played chess every day, and he wore the pin at all times, sideways, like the symbol for infinity.

He seemed happy with his lot, but then the weather had remained surprisingly warm all winter, even for Tucson, Roxie's co-workers had told her. "I imagine that there are shelters in this area," she said, "but I don't know much about them."

"I believe those establishments are quite full this time of year. In fact I'm quite certain of it. I suppose my regular bench will suffice. I'll add another layer of newspapers, perhaps."

"That sounds pretty terrible to me." Roxie imagined the long night, with snow falling on a newspaper-covered Charlie. What if he froze to death? She'd never worried too much about him before, but then it had never snowed before. "Charlie, I think you'd better come home with me until the weather improves."

"With you?" His blue eyes twinkled but he shook his head. "Oh, no, I wouldn't think of causing you any inconvenience."

"No, it'll be okay. The Osborns have a small guest house. You'd have complete privacy there."

"A guest house? I don't remember you mentioning that."

"I don't think about it much. My parents were planning to come out, but now they can't, so why don't you use the space? It'll only go to waste."

"I hate to impose," Charlie said hesitantly.

"You wouldn't be imposing." The more Roxie thought of the idea, the better it sounded. She'd been, she might as well face the fact, lonely. Before they left, the Osborns had introduced her to the neighbors on either side, but they'd kept behind their patio walls for the most part and Roxie had hesitated to intrude considering that she'd be house-sitting for only a year.

Of course there was Como, but she was just an animal, after all. Roxie thought of another argument to persuade Charlie, something to make him feel needed. "You could also help me with Como. She's been acting strange lately, and I'd like a second opinion about whether to call the vet. I don't want to waste the Osborns' money unnecessarily, but on the other hand..."

"Discerning an animal's needs can be difficult, all right. But Roxie, my child, aren't you getting ahead of yourself?

You're speaking as if the matter of my staying in the guest house is settled, yet perhaps the Osborns would object to a common vagrant living on the premises while they're gone."

"You're not a common vagrant. You're my friend. I've known you for six months and we've shared our lunch hour for the past two. I won't have you freezing to death on a park bench tonight when there's a perfectly good place for you to stay until the weather warms up."

"That's kind of you, of course, but—"

"And besides, the Osborns are wonderful people and they'd understand. My parents have known them forever—my dad and Dave Osborn were in the army together. They said anything I wanted to do was fine with them. So let's not discuss it anymore. It's settled."

"My goodness, what a barrage of arguments. Were you by chance a student of debate?"

"Good guess. I was high school debate champion in Newark. So how about it? Have I convinced you to stay with me?"

"Yes, indeed you have." Charlie's wrinkled face creased into a smile. "Bless you, Roxie Lowell."

"Hey, Roxie." A man with dark hair and eyes left the crowd by the window and strolled over to the counter. "Hi, Charlie."

Charlie nodded to the man. "Doug."

"Roxie, everybody's talking about going home early, and I wanted to make sure we were still on for that drink at the Samniego House."

"Gee, Doug, I'm sorry. I forgot about that, with the excitement about the snow and everything."

"A little snow wouldn't stop you, a girl from New Jersey, would it?" He pronounced the name of her home state "New Joisey," as he always did to tease her.

She laughed to humor him, but the joke had become old and she wished he'd find a more clever one. "No, of course the snow won't bother me, but I'm taking Charlie home tonight, because of the bad weather."

Doug's eyebrows shot up. "That's a better offer than you've ever made to me."

"He'll be staying in the guest house," Roxie said pointedly. "Besides," she added with a chuckle, "you're not as sweet as Charlie."

"That's because you won't give me the chance." Doug's glance was half-kidding, half-serious. "Roxie, could I talk to you in private for a minute?" He took her elbow without waiting for a response, and when he'd steered her several feet away from the counter he lowered his voice. "Are you crazy? That old man will become a real leech. Once he's moved into your place you'll never get rid of him, until the Osborns get home, at any rate."

"Doug, stop it. He may hear you."

He shrugged. "So what? He's a bum, a transient."

"Doug!" Roxie grabbed his arm and pulled him farther out of earshot. "Charlie is a wonderful old man and I won't have you downgrading him."

"I guess he is. Otherwise you wouldn't spend every damn lunch hour with him."

She glanced at him in surprise. "You really are jealous of him, aren't you?"

"Not of him—he's an old man—but of the time you spend, yeah, I guess I am."

"I've invited you to join us for lunch."

"No thanks." Doug looked back at Charlie. "All he talks about is history."

"Which I find fascinating. I wouldn't be surprised if he once taught it."

Doug snorted. "Then why isn't he teaching it now? Why does he sleep in the park?"

"I don't know. People have misfortunes. Anyway, why he's homeless doesn't matter. What matters is that it's snowing and I don't want him out all night in bad weather."

"He's probably used to it."

"Oh, really?" Roxie's patience ran out. "I suppose starving people get used to having no food, too?"

"I don't know, but I do know this is not your problem. Anyway, what about the Osborns? What would they think?"

"They told me I could invite anyone I wanted to stay there, my parents or anyone. My parents have decided they can't afford the time, and I don't have any other friends who might—"

"I wouldn't mind moving in for a few weeks." Doug caressed her arm. "I could discover what life is like in the foothills while we became better acquainted, so to speak."

She moved away, annoyed with his touch. But she liked Doug, she told herself, except for his attitude about Charlie. "I wouldn't consider such a thing and you know it. The Osborns don't expect my boyfriends to live there. Besides, you have a roof over your head. Charlie doesn't."

Doug's expression hardened. "Roxie, I'm telling you you're going to regret this. Donating money to charities is one thing. This is something else entirely."

"Yes, it's better." Roxie glared at him defiantly. "By taking Charlie home with me I know someone is being helped by my efforts. I don't have to wonder how my money was spent. I'm doing this, Doug, so don't try to stop me."

Doug raised both hands in a helpless shrug. "My father warned me never to argue with a redhead."

"This has nothing to do with the color of my hair. Now, if you'll excuse me, Charlie and I are going home."

"Does that mean you'll be busy tomorrow night, or are we still going out?" Doug asked with exaggerated courtesy.

She tried to curb her temper. After all, she did care about Doug and he probably had a right to be sarcastic. She had broken their date for tonight because of Charlie, an old man Doug didn't like. "I'll be ready at seven," she said quietly. Then she returned to her desk for her coat and purse and soon joined Charlie in the lobby.

"He doesn't approve of your behavior, does he?" Charlie asked.

"It's none of his business. We're dating, not married."

"Oh, Roxie, I certainly hope you won't consider marriage to Doug Kelly, of all people."

She glanced at him as they walked down the tiled hall of the courts building. "I have considered it, Charlie. He's a nice-looking man with a steady job, and usually we have fun together."

"What about love?"

"I sort of love Doug."

Charlie shook his head sadly.

"Well, I'm working on that part. But I'm twenty-seven, Charlie. Every day couples come into the office to apply for marriage licenses and I envy them. I'm ready to settle down, raise a family. I'd love to have children some day. I'd make a good mother."

"Of course you would." Charlie turned up the worn collar of his tweed coat as they crossed the Pennington Street footbridge and left prints in the thin layer of snow that had collected there. "But Doug Kelly is not the gentleman for you."

"Why not?" Roxie guided Charlie toward the elevator that led to an underground parking garage.

"The reason you don't love Doug yet is that there's not enough love in him to inspire you," he replied as they rode down. "It may not be entirely his fault, of course, with that name. But then, I've known some Kellys who were wonderful lovers. Still and all, in Doug's case…"

"Charlie, what are you talking about?"

"I'm talking about Doug's last name. Kelly means *warrior*. Sometimes that has no effect on people, as I said. I knew an Edmond Kelly who was brimming with love and never picked a fight in his life. But in Doug's case, the name is—well, let us say the name doesn't match at all with yours, Roxie."

"My name?" Roxie unlocked the passenger side of her old Volvo. "What's my name have to do with this?"

Charlie waited until she was seated behind the wheel before answering. "Lowell means *beloved*," he said. "And your behavior is completely congruent with your name. That's one reason that I wanted to…be your friend."

"And you last name is Hartman." She started the car and drove out of the gray cement interior of the garage. Snow splattered the windshield as she stopped to pay the fee, and she turned on the wipers.

"Hartman is relatively straightforward, isn't it? Of course, that's not my real name. But I like the assonance of Charlie Hartman. It will do."

Roxie blinked. *Hartman wasn't his real name?* All at once doubts about her decision to take him in crowded around her. Maybe Doug had been right that giving Charlie a temporary home was a terrible mistake. "Charlie, you're not running from the law or anything, are you?"

"Good gracious no! You have nothing to fear from me, Roxie."

As they left downtown traffic and climbed northward into the foothills of the Santa Catalina Mountains, Roxie thought hard. She took into account the rose that Charlie brought to the office every morning, his impeccable manners and his sage observations. She might be a sap, she decided, but she believed that he was a good man. "Then why aren't you using your real name? Is it hard to pronounce or something?"

"Yes, something like that. Isn't the snow delightful? That prickly pear cactus seems as if it's wearing a white nightcap. The desert looks rather...surprised, wouldn't you say?"

"Yes, it does, at that. Well, this is the street, Calle de Suenos." Roxie flicked on her left-turn signal and waited for southbound traffic to clear.

"Street of dreams. How lovely."

"I should have guessed that you'd know Spanish."

"A little. Ah, you have something under construction on your corner. Looks like a rather large project."

"Yes, the Osborns said there was quite a flap about that because the area is primarily residential, but the general contractor agreed to keep the building to one story so it wouldn't block anyone's view in the neighborhood."

"What will it be?"

"A nursing home, I believe." Roxie saw a gap in the oncoming traffic and prepared to turn.

"The workers don't look too happy about the weather."

"I doubt that they're used to dealing with snow."

"Obviously not, from the way they're rushing about. That's a sturdy-looking chap on the roof. I like the way he holds his shoulders. There's confidence in his manner."

"You can tell all that from this distance? And in the snow?"

"Especially in the snow. He's not cowering in the face of it. Looks like quite a remarkable man, actually."

Roxie made her turn and pulled to the side of the road. "You've got my curiosity aroused. Where is this paragon?"

"Right up there, on the top beam."

"Oh." Roxie peered through the thickening snow to the man standing on the roof of the skeleton building. "He looks a little like a captain at the prow of his ship."

"Exactly. He has an air of command about him. Roxie, compare the stance of that man to your Doug Kelly."

"Doug's an office worker. He's not in construction."

"That's immaterial. Can you imagine Doug standing up there in that pose?"

"No, I guess not." Roxie laughed. "Doug would be huddled somewhere warm with a drink in his hand."

"No doubt. What does that sign over there say? My eyes aren't quite what they used to be."

Reluctantly she took her gaze from the man on the roof. Charlie was right, the man created an intriguing picture silhouetted against the gray sky, his yellow hard hat like a beacon as he urged his crew to cover the building materials before the snow did it for them.

Roxie studied the large sign at the corner of the lot. "It says 'Craddock Design and Construction, Commercial and Residential Builder. Licensed, Bonded and Insured.' Then there's the man's full name at the bottom, Hank Craddock, and a telephone number."

"I'll wager that's him up on the roof."

Roxie glanced back at the man. "Could be."

"Craddock, now there's a name for you."

"Okay, I'll bite. What does Craddock mean?"

Charlie looked at her with a satisfied expression. "Abounding in love."

FOUR DAYS OF RAIN followed the freak snowstorm, throwing Craddock Design and Construction behind schedule on the nursing home. Hank was forced to schedule overtime on Saturday, but his crew didn't mind very much. Working in the unpolluted air and spectacular scenery of the foothills was always a treat and fatter paychecks with the overtime made the job just about perfect for them.

Giving up a Saturday wasn't all that bad, either, especially for the ones who had video recorders to keep track of weekend sports on television. As for families, a few of the guys were childless and the rest had wives at home to take care of the kids. Hank didn't like leaving his two with the housekeeper on the weekends, although he'd had to do it several times in the past two years. Dolores was okay, but she couldn't be expected to love Hilary and Ryan the way he did, the way Sybil had.

Yet he loved his job, too, and inevitably it required a certain amount of weekend work. If he could forget that today was Saturday and the kids would certainly miss having him around, he could enjoy the buzz of the power saws and the echoing crack of the hammers. The sounds meant something new was being created, and he thrived on that knowledge.

Ever since he'd been old enough to play in the mud he'd been building things. He would scrounge bent nails and scrap lumber, confiscate his dad's hammer, and spend all his spare hours making caves for toy dinosaurs, forts for green plastic army men, tunnels and trestles for electric trains. When he'd graduated to power tools he'd redesigned the inside of his bedroom with platforms of different levels and a loft bed that was seven feet off the ground.

He still loved the heft of a good hammer, the precision of a level, the power of a drill. He even loved the smells of construction—the musty scent of disturbed earth, the damp pungency of curing cement, the tang of fresh paint. The nursing home was in the framing stage, and as the whirling saws sliced into board after board, Hank breathed deep of the sweet wood scent.

Every morning he walked the length of the site to compare the progress with the plans he carried in one hand and the ideal he carried in his head. Some people said he had vision, and he liked to think it was true.

On this particular Saturday morning, however, he wondered if he'd developed double vision. As he began walking the north perimeter he saw the oddest couple of sidewalk superintendents he'd come across in fifteen years of working in construction. He stepped through a break in the cyclone fence surrounding the site to have a better look.

The man was an old guy dressed in an out-of-style tweed sport coat and a jaunty, narrow-brimmed hat. The animal he held by a lead rope was... Hank squinted and rummaged through his sparse knowledge of zoological creatures. A llama, for God's sake. A white llama with a coat as luxurious as that of an Angora cat.

The man and the beast went together like peanut brittle and champagne. Either the old guy should have been wearing a sombrero and a serape or the animal on the end of the rope should have been an English terrier. Hank had much to do that day, but he decided he owed it to himself to check out the unlikely pair.

"Good morning," he called when he got within ten yards of the odd couple. "Taking your llama for a walk, I see. Nice day for it."

"She's not my llama, actually, but yes, I'm giving her some exercise. I was also hoping to make the acquaintance of Hank Craddock."

"I'm Hank. But I'll tell you right now that I don't know beans about llamas." Upon closer inspection of the pair

Hank became more curious than ever. The old guy's speech and manner fit the tone of this affluent area, but his dress was pretty shabby. Maybe he'd been hired to exercise the llama, but he was the most unusual exercise boy Hank had ever seen.

"I'm not here seeking advice, Mr. Craddock, about llamas or anything else, for that matter. I merely wanted to offer a few comments."

Hank was used to comments. The residents had put him through his paces over this project, but he didn't remember this particular fellow from those long meetings. "The design of the building's been cleared with the home owners' association, so you'll have to take any complaints to them, I'm afraid."

"Ah, don't get your feathers ruffled, my good man. I have only positive things to say on this fine morning. I don't know much about building," the old fellow continued in his confident tone, "but I know a great deal about people. I've been watching your operation here and I'm impressed with an atmosphere of—dare I call it 'love'?"

Hank frowned. Who did he have here; some sort of religious nut? Maybe the llama was a sacred beast for some obscure cult he hadn't heard about. "I'm not sure what you mean, Mr.—"

"My name is Charlie Hartman. And I mean that there's an air of goodwill surrounding this endeavor. I would venture to say that you love your job, Mr. Craddock, and it shows."

"Why, thank you." Hank tapped the rolled plans nervously against his thigh. The old guy probably was nuttier than a fruitcake, but a compliment was a compliment.

"Perhaps it has something to do with your name."

"My name? No, I don't think so. You see, most of my family still lives in South Dakota and none of them are in construction, anyway. You must be thinking of somebody else named Craddock."

"I'm not talking about your family, but about your family name. Craddock means *abounding in love*. But of course you probably are aware of that."

"No." Hank couldn't remember ever having a stranger conversation, and in front of such a polite audience, besides. The llama was beautifully behaved. It stood quietly staring at him with an occasional blink of its long white eyelashes. "No, I wasn't aware that Craddock meant anything."

"Well, no doubt your wife is. Women often pay more attention to such matters."

"My wife is—" Hank caught himself before he spilled his guts to this crazy old coot. "I'm not married," he finished briefly.

"What a shame." Charlie smiled.

"Yeah, it is." *Crazy as a bedbug*, Hank concluded. "Listen, do you live around here?" If the old man was senile he might have wandered out of his house and hitched up the llama when his wife or his housekeeper weren't looking. He might be lost.

"I'm staying with someone right down the street," Charlie said, pointing. "A lovely young woman named Roxie Lowell. Perhaps you know her? She has flame-red hair, about this long." He drew an imaginary line across the side of his neck. "And charming freckles, and eyes that—well, they remind me of the Mediterranean."

"That's quite a description." This meeting was one for the books, Hank thought. And here he'd thought Calle de Suenos was an ordinary street populated with normal, if somewhat persnickety folks. "Is she your granddaughter?"

"No, just a very dear friend. She's loaning me her guest house temporarily."

"And her llama?"

"In a manner of speaking. Walking an animal is a good excuse to stroll the neighborhood and meet new friends, wouldn't you agree?"

"I—ah—yes." Hank glanced at the llama, whose head was nearly as high as his. "I imagine you'll meet all sorts of people walking this animal."

"Well, I suppose Como and I should be getting back."

"Como? That's her name?"

"Yes, precisely."

"As in Perry?"

"No, as in *Como se llama, llama.* 'Como' for short."

Hank laughed. "'Her name is llama,'" he translated. "Cute."

"I thought it rather clever, too. Well, Como, we'd better go home, hadn't we? Roxie will wonder what's become of us." He scratched the llama's nose and she nuzzled his shoulder. "She's extremely affectionate if she approves of you."

"Your friend Roxie or the llama?"

"Both, actually."

Hank had trouble keeping a straight face. "Can you find your way home okay?"

"Why, certainly. Did you suppose that I was lost?"

"Well, I—" Hank had supposed exactly that.

"It's quite all right. Don't be distressed. Lots of people I meet assume that I'm slightly touched in the head."

"I can't imagine why they would think that." Hank suppressed a grin.

"Neither can I. I assure you that I'm—what's one of the current expressions?—playing with a full deck."

"I'm glad to hear it."

Charlie Hartman tipped his hat. "Good day, Mr. Craddock."

"See you around."

"Yes, you just might, at that." The man tugged on the lead rope. "Come along now, Como."

Hank restrained himself until Charlie was out of earshot and well on his way to the house inhabited by the lovely young woman with flame-red hair and eyes the color of the Mediterranean. And a llama. Mustn't forget the llama, he thought. Finally, as Hank retraced his steps along the north perimeter, he allowed himself the good laugh that he'd held back ever since he'd noticed Charlie Hartman and the llama.

What a funny old guy, Hank thought, still chuckling, and what a commercial he'd given for his hostess. His praise sounded old-fashioned and gallant, sort of like the quaint old fellow himself. Roxie might be all that he'd said, but considering Charlie's age, his idea of a "young woman" might be anyone under sixty. Roxie Lowell could have a multitude of chins and bags under those blue-green eyes. Nevertheless, she certainly had Charlie's complete admiration.

Had Hank been standing on the roof of his building instead of on the ground, he could have satisfied some of his curiosity about Roxie by watching her as she worked inside the Osborns' walled patio. She made use of Como's absence to clean out the stall in the miniature barn the Osborns had constructed for their llama. Then she lined the floor with fresh straw and raked the small corral. Upon finishing that Roxie walked back toward the house and stopped to pick a grapefruit on the way.

She'd taken good care of the fruit trees during the snow-storm, covering them with sheets and warming them with the electric trouble lights the Osborns had left for the purpose. Harvesting the golden fruit each morning had become a cherished ritual, and sharing half with Charlie made her enjoyment complete. As she picked a grapefruit from the nearest branch, Charlie and Como arrived through the side gate.

"What a joyous morning," he said, unbuckling Como's halter and closing her into the corral. "This halcyon weather is reminiscent of Southern Italy."

Roxie welcomed the chance to learn more about him. "You've been there?"

"Oh, yes." Charlie's expression became dreamy. "Of course, Northern Italy is breathtaking, too. I remember how much Romeo and Juliet loved it."

"Romeo and Juliet?" Roxie wondered if he'd just named his children or grandchildren. She hoped not. Only a real nut would give kids names like that. Must be dogs. "Who were Romeo and Juliet?"

He glanced up, as if coming out of a trance. "They were...I suppose in today's vernacular you'd say they were clients. That boy and girl had so much love, but—" He paused and shook his head. "I prefer not to dwell on the sad stories."

"You mean someone actually named their children Romeo and Juliet? I imagine that they *would* have problems, with names like that. Were you some sort of counselor, Charlie?" Roxie wondered if she'd guessed wrong when she'd imagined him as a history professor.

"Yes, a counselor," Charlie said vaguely. "But that was a long time ago. Shall we have some breakfast?" He opened the French door that led into the kitchen. "I want to tell you about Mr. Craddock."

"Who?" Roxie carried the grapefruit to the sink and rinsed it off. Then she placed it on the chopping block and sliced it in half. Each morning she savored the moment when the sharp citrus aroma filled the kitchen.

"Hank Craddock, the chap we saw on the roof the first

day I came here." Charlie hung his fedora on a rack beside the door.

"Oh." Roxie sectioned the grapefruit and thought about the man on the roof. So Charlie had made friends with him already. Not surprising.

"Excellent person," Charlie continued, sitting down at the glass-topped table in the breakfast nook. "Cares for his fellowman. He was afraid that I might be a bit senile and I'll wager that he would have shepherded me home himself if he'd become convinced of it. But I mentioned that I was staying with you and that I was quite sane. We had a nice chat. I also told him about you."

Roxie stopped sectioning and looked at him. "About me? What do you mean, about me?"

"Don't become alarmed. I said only good things."

Roxie became very alarmed indeed. "Like what?"

"I told him you had flame-red hair and eyes the color of the sea. Oh, and I mentioned the freckles, too. He appears to be a man who would appreciate a few freckles."

Roxie put the knife down and turned to face him. "Charlie Hartman, whatever possessed you to do such a thing? I can't believe you walked up to a complete stranger and started raving about how I looked!"

Charlie smiled at her. "I thought he should know. Now he'll think about you while he works."

"I wouldn't doubt it! Charlie, I'm really embarrassed."

He waved one hand. "No need, no need. I didn't say much more about you, really. Only that you were an affectionate sort."

"Oh, my lord."

"You blush so becomingly, but you have no reason to be upset. I only spoke the truth."

"Charlie, can you imagine how that must have sounded to him? He must think you were trying to fix me up!"

"Well, I was." Charlie looked unperturbed at the idea. "I suggest that you take a walk later on this morning and introduce yourself to him. He's quite nice."

"I won't be able to walk past that corner ever again, unless I wear a bag over my head, until that construction job is finished." She gazed at him in exasperation, but he only continued to smile at her in that sweet way that had won her heart months ago when she'd first met him. "Oh, I suppose you meant well, Charlie, but you shouldn't have blabbed about me to some strange man."

"He's not strange. I'm an excellent judge of character and he's someone you should meet."

"Even if that were true, which it probably isn't, I can't possibly meet him after what you've said. Flame-red hair and eyes the color of the sea? Really, Charlie! And then you added that I'm affectionate!"

"Perhaps I overreached my boundaries a bit, but I could see no other recourse."

His nonsensical statements strained Roxie's tolerance and her tone grew a bit sharp. "No other recourse? Would you mind explaining that?"

Charlie folded his arms and looked her straight in the eye. "I had no recourse under our present circumstances."

She threw both hands in the air. "What circumstances?" she asked impatiently. "Charlie, either you're crazy or I am, and I'm betting on you."

"It's very simple, really. Today is Saturday, February eleventh. That makes Tuesday St. Valentine's Day. Roxie, my dear child, we're running out of time."

2

ROXIE STARED AT CHARLIE. "You really scare me when you say things that don't make sense."

"This makes sense if you understand the importance of St. Valentine's Day. You can't trifle with a day like that, Roxie, not when you're focusing on marriage the way you are these days."

"I don't get it. What are you trying to say?"

"I'm trying to warn you, Roxie. When a woman is ready to find a man with whom to share her life, and I'm certain that you are, St. Valentine's Day could determine her whole future. What happens on that day will very likely affect everything."

"I still don't understand."

Charlie shook his head. "It saddens me, the amount of ignorance I find among people in this century concerning St. Valentine's Day. Yet ignorant or not, you'll be ruled by the forces at work."

"Good grief, Charlie, what forces?"

"Dry your hands, my dear, and sit down at the table while I explain this to you."

She did as she was told, although she wasn't sure why. "Okay, explain."

Charlie spoke to her with the patient manner of a teacher confronted with a hopelessly slow pupil. "When you are a woman ready to fall in love, the first eligible man you meet on St. Valentine's Day is destined to become your lover and marry you within the year. There have been rare exceptions, of course, but—''

"Charlie, you can't believe such superstitious nonsense."

He sighed and held up one hand. "That's not a very helpful attitude, Roxie. I caution you not to take what I'm saying lightly. You'll rue the day if you don't pay strict attention to what I'm telling you."

Roxie didn't believe a word he was saying, but she couldn't bear to hurt his feelings by telling him so. Bless his heart, he believed that St. Valentine's Day had some mystical significance, and he sincerely wanted to help her find happiness. "Okay, Charlie, I'll pay attention."

He rubbed his hands and smiled. "Good, good. Now, what worries me is that Tuesday is a work day. The first eligible man you're likely to meet will be that weasel-faced Doug Kelly."

"Weasel-faced? That's a terrible thing to say about Doug. He's quite attractive. I could do far worse." Not that she put any faith in this business, she reminded herself.

"I doubt if you could do much worse." Charlie took his handkerchief out and polished his gold pin. "Now take that Craddock fellow I met today. There's a face you can trust. Honest eyes, gray, as I recall, steady gaze. Those eyes can look at a bare patch of ground and imagine something wonderful built there. That's a quality to admire, Roxie."

"Charlie, listen." Roxie put a hand on his arm. "It's sweet of you to take an interest in my love life, and I'm sure this Craddock man is very nice, but I don't know him and I'm not about to saunter down there to meet him, either. If he's like most wonderful men, he's already married, anyway."

"No, he's unattached at the moment."

Roxie gasped. "You asked him?"

"Subtly, of course."

"Charlie, you're about as subtle as a Mack truck."

"I beg your pardon? I've heard of McDonald's, but not McTruck. Is it some new fast-food chain?"

Roxie controlled her laughter. "No, it's—never mind. I guess you don't know quite everything, Charlie. And when it comes to my love life, you're really uninformed. Doug may not be able to look at a bare piece of ground and envision a wonderful structure on it, but he likes me a lot and he's available."

"He may be available but he doesn't have the capacity to appreciate you. Hank Craddock, on the other hand—"

"Listen, I don't care what your Mr. Craddock told you, he could still be married. I've learned that men don't always tell the truth in these matters, but I've checked on Doug, and he has no wife stashed anywhere."

"Hank wasn't lying to me. Not with that strong face and those capable hands."

Roxie decided the time had come for some revelations. "Charlie, wake up. I fell for a guy back in New Jersey who had the most trustworthy face you'd ever imagine. For three long years he convinced me that we couldn't get married because he hadn't achieved enough success with his business. Newark's a big city, and he almost got away with it, but one day by a wild coincidence I met his wife."

Charlie accepted the news with a sigh. "I'm so sorry, Roxie." He reached over and patted her hand. "I suspected that you'd been disappointed in love. It gives your eyes a certain depth. Your character, too. But don't let that experience jade you."

"I don't think I'm jaded, but I sure am careful until I know for sure that someone's single."

Charlie nodded. "I understand. It's those kind of fellows who give love a bad name. So I assume you left him straightaway?"

"I knew that was the thing to do." She paused and

glanced at Charlie. This was the tough part to admit, but he might as well know how weak she was. "He wanted to keep on anyway, despite the marriage. He used the old story that his wife would never give him a divorce but that he loved only me."

"You told him what he could do with that dastardly plan, I hope?"

"Well, yes, but...the truth is I was really in love with the jerk. Being in Newark, where I could see him anytime I wanted—well, anytime he wasn't with his wife—I was tempted to go along with the idea, Charlie. I had to leave town in order to get him out of my system."

"Ah. So that's why you came here."

"Yes, and I was lucky to have the chance. When I heard my parents' friends needed a house-sitter, or in this case a llama-sitter while they spent a year in the Orient, I jumped at the opportunity."

"Do you still think of him?"

She paused. "In the first few weeks I thought of him all the time. Now just once in a while. The distance and months apart have shown me how selfish he was and I've lost my respect for him along with my love. But you'll have to forgive me if I'm suspicious of wonderful men who claim to be unmarried."

"I still say you should give Hank Craddock a chance."

Roxie smiled and pushed back her chair. "Let's have some grapefruit."

"You know, on the way to work Tuesday morning, to humor an old man you could stop by the construction site, just for a moment."

"Charlie, give it a rest." She stood and walked to the sink. "Would you like your regular bran cereal this morning or perhaps some eggs?"

"I'd better stick with the bran. It's better for an old man like me."

"You're not so old, Charlie."

"Older than you think."

She hated to see him looking so deflated and she searched for another topic to make him forget his daydreaming about her and Hank Craddock. "Do you think anything's wrong with Como? Does she seem listless or is it just my imagination?"

Charlie snapped his fingers. "Yes, Como. I do know what her problem is."

"What?"

"She's lovesick."

"Oh, Charlie." Roxie shook her head and poured cereal into a bowl. "You've got love on the brain."

"So does Como. She's a lonely llama."

Roxie chuckled. "Well, she's going to have to stay that way until the Osborns come home." She took the milk from the refrigerator and popped some wheat bread into the toaster. "Fixing up Como's love life isn't my responsibility. Now that I think of it, Fran did mention that they'd tried to mate Como but nothing happened. She was too young."

"There are other llamas in Tucson?"

"I guess so."

"Then we'd better make sure she doesn't get out of the patio unless she has a halter and lead rope on."

"I suppose you're right." Roxie noticed that Charlie had used the word *we*, and she liked that. Despite his eccentric behavior with the contractor down the street, Charlie had been welcome company for her and she hoped he'd stay awhile. She'd arrived in Tucson with her self-confidence in shreds. Landing a job in the county clerk's office had begun the repair job on her self-esteem; the promotion to day shift after only four months had continued the process.

As weeks had passed and no disasters had befallen the Osborns' house or their pet llama, she had nurtured a belief in her own judgement, and the strength of that belief had allowed her to take Charlie in. Caring for him gave her life greater purpose, and she sometimes wondered if she needed Charlie more than he needed her.

She took the toast out and spread it with peanut butter. "Maybe I'll get the vet out here, to make sure there isn't something we ought to know about the situation," she said, adopting Charlie's use of the word *we*. "In fact, I'd better call right now, considering how busy he usually is. I think they're open on Saturday mornings."

"Good idea." Charlie got up from the table. "You call and I'll finish the breakfast preparations. Do you want strawberry or cherry jam on your peanut butter toast?"

"Cherry, please." She picked up the receiver of the wall phone in the kitchen and dialed the number that was on the Osborns' list taped up beside the telephone.

When she'd finished talking to the secretary, she turned to Charlie with a smile. "Looks like I won't be seeing Doug Kelly on the morning of St. Valentine's Day. Dr. Babcock is free Tuesday morning and then he'll be out of town for two weeks, so I had to grab him when I could. I'll stay home from work that morning and go in at one o'clock."

A look of panic crossed Charlie's face. "What time is he coming over?"

"The appointment's for ten."

"Is this Dr. Babcock married?"

Roxie laughed. "I have no idea. Really, Charlie, aren't we carrying this a bit too far?"

Charlie mumbled something she couldn't understand and reached for the coffee.

"What did you say?"

"Um, nothing, my dear," he said, pouring two mugs full. "I'll take care of—that is, everything will be fine, just fine."

AT FIVE-THIRTY on Tuesday morning Hank was cruising the aisles of the grocery store and wondering how working parents had survived before the days of the twenty-four-hour supermarket. Hilary had announced fifteen minutes earlier that she was short on valentines for her class. She had refused to go to school unless she had one for every third grader in the room, plus the little boy in fourth grade that she had a tremendous crush on.

Ryan had been no help, either. He'd used up all of his valentines and Hilary hadn't liked the kind he'd bought, anyway. So here Hank stood in front of the picked-over valentine display trying to decide which designs would tickle Hilary's fancy. He finally chose a package that featured lots of cuddly animals. That was Hilary, all right.

He tossed the package into the cart next to the milk and orange juice. Perhaps he should buy Hilary and Ryan each a valentine from him, he thought. Sybil used to do that kind of thing. He wheeled the cart down the deserted aisle to the rack for individual cards and forced his gaze quickly past the valentines that announced they were "For My Wife." Eventually he found the son and daughter cards.

They were pretty stereotyped, he thought, with the daughter cards covered with ruffles and the son cards big on sports themes. Sybil wouldn't have bought this kind at all, Hank realized. She'd probably have found two clever valentines that made no reference to son or daughter but were uniquely suited to the personalities of Ryan and Hilary.

But Sybil wasn't here. With a sigh Hank chose a pink-and-white lacy card for Hilary and one with a boy wielding a baseball bat for Ryan. They'd each like their cards, he knew, because despite all Sybil's efforts and his own attempts to carry out her wishes, Hilary loved dancing and dolls and Ryan loved sports and erector sets.

Hank signed both cards at the checkout counter so that he'd be ready to give them to the kids when he walked in the house. Later, when they met him at the door and thrust out homemade valentines for him, he was glad that he was prepared.

"Happy Valentine's Day, Daddy," Hilary said, hugging him around the waist.

"Happy Valentine's Day, Dad." Ryan's hug was quicker and more awkward. Lately the only prolonged physical contact Ryan allowed himself with anyone was while he was practicing wrestling holds. Hank wrestled with him every time Ryan asked him, suspecting that Ryan needed the closeness although his son had concluded that it was no longer a manly thing to want.

Hank put down the grocery bag on the hall table and read both their valentines before he took off his jacket. Hilary's was decorated with hearts and flourishes and was painstakingly inscribed "To the best Daddy in the world, Happy Valentine's Day." Ryan's had a lopsided heart drawn on the outside, and inside he'd scrawled "To a guy who measures (get it?) up. Love, Ryan."

Pressure built behind his eyes, pressure that would become tears if he'd let them fall. But his kids wouldn't appreciate having Dad cry over their valentines. He cleared his throat and grinned. "What a couple of card makers I have! These are terrific, kids."

"Did you get the joke on mine, Dad? 'Measures up,' like in using a tape measure."

"You bet I got it. Very clever, Ryan."

"Did you like mine, Daddy? Didn't you think it was beautiful?"

"As beautiful as you, sweetheart."

"I'm not beautiful. My hair is plain brown. Why did I have to get plain brown and Ryan got blond like Mommy's? It's not fair."

"It's not 'plain brown.' It's a lovely brunette," Hank said patiently, hoping she didn't have a bottle of peroxide in her room this very minute. "It looks wonderful on you, Hilary."

"No, it doesn't. Brown looks good on you, Daddy, but not on me."

Hank knew what she wanted; she wanted to look like her mother. He was secretly glad that she didn't. It was less painful that way.

"Well, in this bag I have a valentine for a beautiful brunette. Shall I give it to someone else?"

Hilary laughed. "No! I want it, Daddy."

Hank passed out the two valentines and watched the smiles on his children's faces as they read the messages inside. He congratulated himself on thinking of buying the cards. Maybe he wasn't so terrible at this single parenthood business, after all. But that didn't mean he had to like it.

The rest of his morning promised to be less satisfying than the giving of valentines to his kids. Upon arriving at the construction site he discovered that several of the windows that had been delivered were the wrong size. As he walked outside the fence to contact the glass company on the mobile telephone in his truck, he spotted the old man and his llama. Hank didn't want to be rude, but he wasn't in the mood for any more conversation about the woman with flame-red hair and eyes the color of the Mediterranean Sea. Not today.

"Happy St. Valentine's Day," the old man called out in greeting as he approached.

"Same to you. Listen, Mr. Hartman, I've got a major problem here, so if you'll excuse me I have a call to make."

"But I don't see a telephone."

"I have one in my truck."

"Ah."

Hoping that the old man would take the hint, Hank walked faster across the rutted ground. But when he climbed into his truck and closed the door, he glanced back and saw them still coming toward him. He tossed his hard hat on the seat and thumbed through the business cards in his wallet for the glass company's telephone number.

After he'd found it he looked up to find the old man and the llama, their heads about even, framed in the window of the truck, their noses nearly touching the glass. The old man smiled. Hank thought the llama smiled, too.

Hank nodded curtly, not wanting to encourage them in their determined friendliness. He picked up the mobile telephone and listened for the dial tone. Nothing. Muttering an oath he punched the Hang-up button several times and heard some crackling noises but still no dial tone.

The old man tapped on the window and Hank rolled it down. "Yes?"

"You seem to be having several problems, Mr. Craddock."

"A few." Hank drew back as the llama poked her head into the cab. "She doesn't bite, does she?"

"No. If she doesn't like someone she spits on them."

"Wonderful."

"But you don't have to worry. She likes you."

"That's great. Say, could you get her out of here, please? I have windows that don't fit and a dead telephone. I have to locate a pay phone and straighten this out before we end up behind schedule again."

"Why not use Roxie's telephone?" the old man suggested immediately. "It's only a block away. I'm certain she'd be delighted to help."

Hank gazed at him and considered the suggestion for a moment. "Okay. Sure, why not? I'll drive down there, if you don't mind. It'll be faster. She's home, then?"

"Yes... 4335 Calle de Suenos. Arched windows overhung with masses of bougainvillea blossoms."

"Fine. Thanks." Hank couldn't care less about landscaping at this point, but he sure needed a working telephone. The glass company was a good thirty miles through heavy traffic from here, and he wasn't about to make the trip if he could avoid it.

He started the engine and backed onto the street. The old man had come up with a good suggestion at that. The nearest pay phone was at least three miles down the road at a 7-11, and every time Hank had driven past it the telephone had been tied up.

He found the address with no trouble and pulled into the circular drive. Charlie Hartman's benefactress had some bucks, all right. A custom-built home in the foothills hadn't come cheap. As Hank rang the doorbell he prepared himself for a fiftyish woman with dyed-red hair and too much makeup.

When no one answered the bell he rang again and finally heard the front lock click. Then the heavy carved door opened and he was face to face with flame-red hair and eyes that were, indeed, the blue-green of the sea. Hank didn't know exactly what the Mediterranean looked like, but when he looked into Roxie's eyes he thought of lazy days in Mazatlan, so Charlie's description must be about right.

"So he did it," she said.

"I beg your pardon?"

"He got you down here before the vet arrived. How did he do it?"

Hank frowned in bewilderment. "Lady, I don't have the faintest idea what you mean."

"Aren't you Hank Craddock?"

"Yes, and I was wondering if—"

"Charlie sent you down here, didn't he?"

"Yes, but I—"

Then she laughed, drawing his attention to her soft pink mouth and even teeth. She was a beauty, all right, just as Charlie had described her. And both she and Charlie were nuts. "You might as well come in, Mr. Craddock," she said, stepping back from the door. "I'm afraid this is bigger than both of us."

"Listen, could I use your phone?" Hank decided to take charge before he found himself in the Twilight Zone. "The mobile phone in my truck went out and I have to change a glass order."

"What a coincidence." Still smiling, she beckoned him into the house. "Sure, you can use the phone. The closest one's in the den."

He followed her down a tiled hallway and noticed that the top of her head came to his chin, making her about five seven. A nice height. A nice height for what? he asked himself immediately. If she indeed owned this house, at her young age, she had to be a whiz kid career woman or an heiress, and he didn't think he'd be comfortable with either one.

Inside the den she gestured toward a telephone on a sleek oak desk. "Help yourself. I'll be in the kitchen."

"Thanks." As she started to leave he had the crazy wish to continue the conversation somehow. The urgency of his business was beginning to wane in the glow of her fresh beauty. He liked the way she wore her hair, prim and brushed back from her forehead on top, and luxurious, touch-me fullness at the sides and back. "You should have heard how Charlie talked about you," he blurted and then cursed himself for such an obvious line.

She flushed slightly. "He told me what he'd said. You have to excuse Charlie. He means well, but he—"

"Underrated you," Hank shocked himself by saying. "Uh, what I meant to say was that he didn't mention that you were so young." *Not true, Hank, old buddy. He said she was a lovely young lady and you wouldn't believe him.*

"It's the freckles. I'm not as young as you think. I'm twenty-seven."

He smiled at the way she said it, as if she were admitting a terrible secret. Well, when he was twenty-seven he'd thought he was pretty old, too. She was right, though; the freckles and also the high, smooth forehead took off at least five years. "That accent," he said. "You're not from around here, are you?"

She shook her head and her hair rippled with the motion. "Newark, New Jersey."

"What brings you to Tucson?" After he asked the personal question he winced and waited for her to tell him to mind his own business, which he wasn't minding at all at the moment. But once he'd made his call he'd have no excuse to hang around and any opportunity to learn about her would be gone.

For some unfathomable reason she answered his question. "Some friends asked me to house-sit for them."

He grinned with relief. "And here I thought you might be an heiress."

"Hardly," she said, smiling back.

A knot of tension dissolved in him, and he realized that he'd unconsciously placed her out of reach, but now she wasn't at all. A quick glance at her left hand told him what he needed to know, and he began to imagine taking her out to dinner and maybe dancing.

Hank liked dancing although he was a little out of practice. In his dating years before he'd met Sybil, dancing had provided a socially acceptable reason to be close to someone and discover if her body fit with his. Just eyeing the situation Hank thought he and Roxie would dovetail very nicely, but it wouldn't hurt to lead her through a dance or two and make sure.

"Have you ever tried country swing?" he asked. At her puzzled look he realized that he'd made a quantum leap forward in the conversation. "It's a kind of dance people do out here," he explained, trying to sound like a tour guide and not some stud trying to make a move on her. "It's interesting to watch, and I—"

She smiled and laid a hand on his arm. "You don't have to ask me out, you know. Charlie probably begged you to, but don't feel under an obligation to save Roxie from weasel-faced Doug Kelly."

"Who?" He experienced her brief touch as he might the chance landing of an exotic butterfly. He didn't move a muscle to disturb the contact. When she took her hand away and frowned, he sighed with regret.

"Charlie didn't mention him, and the St. Valentine's Day legend?" she asked.

"Look, apparently you know a lot more than I do about this situation. All I know is that Charlie happened to be there when my phone went out this morning, and he suggested I come down here to make my call."

"Which you haven't made yet," she reminded him gently.

"You're right. Maybe I should do that, so the windows can be on their way, and then you can tell me about weasel-faced Doug Kelly and Valentine's Day. It sounds like an interesting story." There. He'd left the door open for more conversation after the call.

"No, it's very dull, and I shouldn't have opened my big mouth. I just thought, when you brought up dancing, that Charlie had talked you into asking me out."

"Charlie didn't mention it, but that doesn't mean it isn't an appealing idea." He decided to go for broke. "Would you like to sometime?"

"I—we'll see. Make your call."

"Okay." He fumbled for the wallet in his back pocket and dropped it, spilling pictures and business cards on the Oriental rug under their feet. "Well, damn." He stooped immediately to retrieve everything.

"Accidents happen," she said, bending to help him.

Hank enjoyed the excuse to be near her. Most women he knew smelled good, but no two had exactly the same scent. Roxie's was light and spicy; it fit. "I haven't managed a stunt like this in years," Hank said. "Not since the night I was trying to use a fake ID to get a drink at the Wildcat House."

She didn't laugh or respond at all, and he glanced up in surprise. Then he stood and frowned in confusion as she silently handed him the stuff she'd retrieved. The come-hither expression had completely vanished from her face and in its place was the blank stare of a woman who could have been in a scene from Madame Tussaud's Wax Museum.

"Is something wrong?" he asked.

"Nothing that I wouldn't have expected, Mr. Craddock. And no, I don't think we'll be going out."

"I don't understand."

"Never mind. If you'll excuse me, I'm going to make myself a cup of hot coffee. You can lock the front door on your way out." She turned and left the room.

Hank couldn't believe the abrupt change in her. One minute she'd been open and filled with good humor, ready to laugh about her friend Charlie's manipulations and possibly consider a date with him. Then she'd pulled back with the speed of a steel tape measure. What had he done?

Shaking his head, he shoved the stuff back in his wallet except the card for the glass company. What a strange lady, this Roxie Lowell from Newark. Just when he'd begun to think the chemistry was working between them, she'd made a complete about-face.

Probably his approach was rusty. After all, he'd only dated a couple of women in the past two years, and they both had been women he'd known for a long time. He hadn't needed an approach with them, but after an attempt at physical intimacy in both cases, Hank had decided that the necessary excitement was missing and neither relationship was destined to go beyond the friendship stage. Yet the minute he'd seen Roxie Lowell this morning, his response had been a whole different story.

Somehow he'd muffed his chance with her, though. With a shake of his head he picked up the telephone and dialed the number of the glass company. After handling his business with them, he walked quietly out of the house and locked the door behind him.

A few minutes later Roxie was still sitting in the sunny kitchen sipping her coffee and trying to contain her anger when Charlie came in, all smiles and winks.

"What did you think of him?" he asked as if certain of the answer.

"You were right about his looks. He's a handsome devil, all right."

"And?"

"And nothing. He's married."

"He most certainly is not. He's not wearing a wedding

band. I ascertained that detail this morning before I directed him over here."

"Then how do you explain the picture in his wallet of him with a blond woman and two children that look very much like both of them?"

Charlie's eyes widened. "Roxie Lowell, you didn't go through his wallet, did you?"

"No, he made things very easy for me. He dropped his wallet on the floor and I helped him pick everything up. That's how I saw the picture."

"But he told me that he wasn't married. He could be divorced, you know."

"Maybe, but divorced men usually don't carry pictures of their ex-wives in their wallets. I know one man who cut his ex-wife's face right out of the family portrait because he still wanted to look at the kids, but not her."

Charlie tapped his chin with his forefinger. "I can't believe that I'm wrong about this man, but let's find out for certain." He walked to the shelf under the kitchen telephone and took out the directory.

"What are you going to do?"

"Call his house and ask for Mrs. Craddock."

"And then what if she comes to the phone?"

"I'll try to sell her carpet cleaning or solar heat. Don't worry. I'll ad lib."

Roxie put down her mug and stood. "If you're really going to do this let me listen in on the extension."

"Just don't cough or anything, my dear, or the jig's up."

"I won't. I'll go in the den. Call me when it's ringing and I'll pick up my line."

She walked back into the room where Hank had been only moments before, and her skin prickled at the memory of his presence there. The outdoor nature of his job and his healthy tan had given him a physical aura that was missing from the other men she'd known. The windswept freedom he'd brought into the room lingered, tempting her still.

Charlie had been right about his eyes; they reflected a vision of structures yet to be created, designs yet to be dreamed of. Roxie also had enjoyed the glint of interest when he'd looked at her. She'd been willing to believe that he wasn't married, that perhaps Charlie had found her a valentine after all, until the picture had fallen out of his wallet.

"It's ringing!" Charlie called from the kitchen.

Roxie picked up the telephone receiver and remembered that Hank's lips had been as close to the mouthpiece as hers were now. She'd seldom looked at a man upon first meeting him and wondered what his kiss would be like, but she'd done that today with Hank.

The phone stopped ringing and a woman with a Spanish accent answered. The accent caused Roxie to dismiss her immediately as the maid. The woman in the picture had been Anglo-Saxon without a doubt.

Charlie spoke with smooth confidence. "May I speak with Mrs. Hank Craddock, please? It's extremely important."

In the pause that followed, Roxie felt a sneeze coming and pushed her finger against the base of her nose to stop it.

"There is no Mrs. Craddock," the woman said.

"I beg your pardon?" Charlie responded. "There must be some mistake. Mrs. Craddock has been recommended to chair the Roses and Rhapsody Charity Ball for Tucson's underprivileged children."

Roxie listened with a smile to Charlie's imaginative line. One thing was for sure, Charlie was never dull. Over the weekend she'd washed a few of his things for him and had discovered that he wore undershorts decorated with red hearts.

"I think the mistake is yours, sir," the woman said in her soft musical voice. "You see, Mrs. Craddock passed away two years ago."

Roxie gasped and immediately clapped her hand over the mouthpiece. Then she gently lowered the receiver to its cradle without bothering to listen in on Charlie's apologies to the woman for disturbing her. Died! His blond wife in the picture had died! The thought had never occurred to her that someone so young...

Roxie bit her lip. Those poor children. In the picture they'd looked small and vulnerable—still in elementary school. Thank goodness they had a father like Hank, who seemed to be a caring, generous man. She cringed at the way she'd treated him, and of course he had no idea why she would be so rude.

"Does that answer your question?" Charlie leaned in the doorway of the den and gazed at her.

"I feel awful. After I'd seen the picture I was really nasty to him. He has to think that I'm a shrew."

"Perhaps I'll meander down there later today and repair the damage."

"No! I mean, that would seem so—oh, I don't know what to do. By now he probably thinks that both you and I are lunatics." She slumped to the leather desk chair. "A reasonable person would have asked him about that picture, instead of assuming the worst. After the way I was tricked before, I had a knee-jerk reaction."

"It doesn't matter. I'll talk to him and explain."

"Charlie, that doesn't seem like enough, somehow. I don't want you running down there and apologizing as if I were some wayward child. I should be the one making the apology, except that I'd be embarrassed, in front of all those men working with him."

"Let me talk to him, then," Charlie suggested again.

"No, I have a better idea." She opened a desk drawer and rummaged in it for paper and a pen. "If you'll deliver it, I'll write him a note. I'll ask his forgiveness for my rude behavior, and I'll—I know—invite him to bring his children over for supper on Saturday night, to see Como. How's that?"

Charlie walked over to the desk and peered at the blank sheet of paper. "I was thinking more of a candlelit dinner for two, with some soft music in the background, and—"

Roxie shook her head. "You're talking about a scene that would spell only one thing to some men. I'm not starting out a relationship that way. I'm not even sure I'm starting a relationship. After all, he has children, and I don't have any experience dating a man with children."

"You didn't have any experience with the county clerk's office, either, and you were promoted in four months."

"That's hardly the same thing," she said with a chuckle.

"No, but I know that you're flexible and intelligent, and of course loving. You'll be fine with those children."

"Charlie, you're way ahead of yourself, here. But no doubt about it, some sort of apology is called for and dinner for Hank and his kids seems like the answer."

"But if you started out getting to know each other first, then—"

"Look." She glanced up at him in exasperation. "It's the note for supper with his kids or nothing. You don't understand the modern ways, Charlie. If I invited him for a candlelit dinner in the dining room he might expect the evening to end in the bedroom, and I don't want even a hint of that. I'm not the kind of woman who likes to move that fast."

Charlie stepped back in surprise. "Good gracious, I didn't expect you to! Maybe I have a few things to learn about the courtship rituals nowadays. I only thought you two could become better acquainted if you were alone."

"We may not become acquainted at all, after what happened this morning. He may refuse my invitation for Saturday night."

Charlie smiled mysteriously. "Oh, I don't think so."

"He might. I wounded his ego, and men don't like that."

"A man like Hank can rise above a wounded ego. I knew that when I—well, anyway, don't forget the most important aspect of this morning's meeting."

"What's that?"

"The die has been cast, and for all intents and purposes your romantic future is set."

"I hardly think so, Charlie," she protested automatically, although when she thought about Hank, she began to doubt logic. Something about the look in his gray eyes made her wonder if—strange as it seemed—Charlie could be right.

3

ROXIE WROTE FOUR VERSIONS of her apology-invitation note before she was satisfied enough to let Charlie take it down the street to Hank Craddock. He made the trip without Como this time, because the vet was due any minute. By the time Charlie returned, carrying what looked like a piece of scrap lumber from the construction site, Roxie was waving goodbye to Dr. Babcock as he pulled out of the circular drive.

She stood by the open front door and waited for Charlie to reach her. Viewing the scrap lumber, she hoped that his hand-to-mouth existence hadn't turned him into a scavenger. She couldn't have junk piling up around the Osborns' house.

"What's the prognosis?" he called as he approached.

"Charlie, I'm not sure you should pick up that kind of thing. We have enough firewood, and I—"

"Oh, you misunderstand, my dear." He handed her the two-foot length of pine. "This is your reply from Hank."

"The guy couldn't find paper?"

"Read the message and you'll understand."

Roxie looked at the words printed neatly in ballpoint pen. "Charlie, that's so corny!"

"Perhaps, but considering that your missive caught him by surprise, I'd say he did quite well on short notice."

Roxie read the words again, this time out loud. "'I'll never be "board" with you. Be my Valentine.' What a terrible pun," she said with a grin. She didn't want to admit to Charlie how much Hank's gesture pleased her, perhaps because it was silly. Chancing something like this with a woman he barely knew showed courage and a sense of fun.

"The rest of his reply is on the other side," Charlie said.

Roxie turned the board over. "Don't worry about this morning," he'd written. "Misunderstandings happen. We'd love to accept your supper invitation. Hank." She glanced at Charlie, who had his hands behind his back and was rocking on his heels with a satisfied smile on his face. "Proud of yourself?" she asked.

"Infinitely. By the way, I gave him your telephone number, in the event he needs to call you. I hope that's agreeable with you."

Roxie shrugged. "Why not? Why fight city hall?"

"Fight who?"

"It's an expression that means if you can't beat 'em, join 'em. Really, Charlie, you need to brush up on your slang. Sometimes you act as if you don't quite belong in this century."

"Sometimes I wonder what I'm doing here, myself."

"What?"

"Never mind, my dear, never mind. Are you going to send him a valentine back?"

"Why, I hadn't thought of it," she fibbed, glancing down the street toward the sounds of electric saws and nail guns. "Besides, I'd have a hard time topping this." She held up the board.

"Maybe something will come to you. In the meantime, let's go inside," Charlie said, taking her elbow in a courtly gesture. "All this walking has worn out these tired old bones. We can sit in the kitchen while you tell me about the veterinarian's visit. Did you happen to notice if he wore a wedding ring?"

"Yes, I did," Roxie replied as they reentered the house. "But only because you've made me buggy on the subject. He does."

"Well, one can never be too careful. It's been a good morning's work, nonetheless."

Roxie shook her head in amazement. "Anyone would think you engineered the whole thing. It was just coincidence that I happened to be home today when Hank's mobile phone went out. And you happened to be there at the right time. Coincidence, plain and simple."

Charlie settled into his favorite kitchen chair and opened his mouth as if to say something. Then he closed it again.

"You were about to tell me this is all the magic of St. Valentine's Day, weren't you?" Roxie accused.

"Something like that."

Roxie poured herself and Charlie a glass of cold water from the bottle she kept chilled in the refrigerator. She'd discovered soon after her arrival that Tucson tap water was lukewarm. "Face it, Charlie; I'm a logical person who likes dealing with facts, not myths. That's probably why I've done well in the clerk's office." She smiled teasingly as she handed him the glass and sat down at the table. "And beat you almost every night in chess."

"Ah, but I've had you on the ropes several times."

"Yes, but who wins?"

Charlie sipped his water. "You, my dear, but then it's so delightful to watch your eyes sparkle in victory, that I don't mind losing."

"Oh, Charlie." She laughed and squeezed his hand. "You're such an old sweetheart."

"I certainly try. And while we're on the subject of sweethearts, how's our Como?"

"Well, you were right. Poor Como needs a boyfriend, but I'm afraid she'll have to wait until the Osborns get back. I'm a city girl, and even if the Osborns gave me the go-ahead I'm not ready to play Cupid for a llama. Too risky."

"Do you think the Osborns might approve such a course of action?" Charlie showed interest in the possibility.

"Charlie, now stop it." Roxie got up and rinsed her glass at the sink. "Be satisfied with your human matchmaking, okay? That could get us in enough trouble without adding in llama love."

"But—"

"No, Charlie." She picked up the scrap of wood on the kitchen counter and waved it at him. "This is enough mischief for one day. End of discussion."

"Just remember that you're holding the most important valentine you'll receive today, perhaps ever. I hope you'll treasure it."

"Shall I sleep with it under my pillow tonight?"

"Perhaps."

"Charlie, I wasn't serious."

"Give yourself time, Roxie, and you will be. Don't throw that wood away, in any case."

Roxie glanced at the unfinished length of two-by-four in her hand. "Okay, but you sure make life tough for a girl, Charlie. I'll have a heck of a time pasting this in my scrapbook."

"You have a scrapbook?"

"No. I was kidding about that, too."

"My, my." Charlie shook his head. "Such a lack of sentiment in this day and age. Well, have you decided what you are going to send him back? That would round out the day quite nicely."

"I can't imagine what. Excuse me a minute, Charlie, but I need to call the office and tell them that I'll definitely be in this afternoon." She reached for the kitchen phone and then pulled her hand back. "That's it!"

"What is?"

"My valentine to Hank." She dashed into her bedroom for her purse. "I have to go buy it," she explained quickly to Charlie on her way back through the kitchen. "Keep your fingers crossed that they have one in stock."

"Crossed fingers won't work if I don't know what I'm crossing them for, Roxie. Anybody knows that."

"Never mind. I'll tell you about it later," she said, opening the side door into the garage. "Please fix us a couple of sandwiches and I'll be back in a jiffy."

"Glad to, my dear." Charlie smiled at her. "And you'll be delivering this valentine in person, then?"

"That's the only way to do it, with this thing."

Charlie's smile widened. "Capital, just capital."

As she drove to the chocolate shop, Roxie thought about Charlie's determined effort to bring Hank into her life. She wasn't sure what Charlie was getting out of all this, but perhaps seeing young people happy made his own lonely situation easier to bear.

Roxie was beginning to wonder what she'd do about Charlie when she had to move into her own place after the Osborns returned. After only a few days with the old gentleman she couldn't imagine turning him out into the world again. Yet she'd considered buying a town house or condo, which wouldn't leave much extra money to feed Charlie. Maybe taking him in and becoming attached to him hadn't been a very logical move.

Still, she had time to come up with some answers. The Osborns wouldn't be home for six months, and lots could happen in six months. According to Charlie, her future had begun to change when she met Hank this morning. And sure enough here she was, dashing off to buy something easily as silly, and much more costly, than his "board" valentine. Oh, well, she thought, at least his kids would love it.

After she'd left the chocolate shop with her purchase, she remembered Doug. He would certainly give her something for Valentine's Day and she hadn't bought him so much as a card. In addition to that, she'd made a sort of date with a man—even if he was bringing his children—for Saturday night. She and Doug had spent nearly every Saturday night together for the past three months.

She tried to work up some remorse for ignoring Doug this way, but slowly she realized that she'd grown tired of him. She was tired of the way he always pronounced "New Joisey" to make fun of her accent, tired of his disdain for Charlie and mostly tired of his self-absorbed attitude toward life.

Perhaps it took someone like Hank to expand her vision, she thought. Today Doug's spirit appeared small and mean compared to that of a man raising two children by himself, a man who had treated Charlie with courtesy and caring, a man not afraid to send her a message written on a piece of scrap lumber. No, she hadn't any desire to send Doug Kelly a valentine.

Roxie parked her car outside the fence and glanced around for Hank. When she couldn't spot him right away she knew she'd have to ask, which would make her a darn sight more conspicuous than she wanted to be. But she had to unload this valentine quickly. It might be melting already.

Roxie picked up the box from the seat beside her and got out of the car. The all-male crew intent on tasks that she didn't understand intimidated her, but she tried not to show it while walking across the rutted ground corrugated by countless truck and tractor tires. She was thankful she'd decided to deliver Hank's valentine before changing into high heels and the rest of her office garb.

After stopping to let a forklift pass she picked out an approachable-looking man and headed toward him. Several members of the crew had paused momentarily to stare at her, and she was aware of every curious look. Once word got around that she'd come to see Hank, he probably wouldn't have a minute's peace with these fellows, she thought. But then, he seemed like a man who could take that kind of teasing. She hoped so. She hadn't intended to embarrass him.

The worker she'd chosen to question was fitting a window into an opening. When he caught sight of her he took the window down and leaned it gently against the studs along what would be the outside wall. "Can I help you?" he asked pleasantly.

She was grateful for his congenial question and wondered if Hank had anything to do with the manners of the people he hired. If this one was an example, they were nice guys. "I'm looking for Hank Craddock," she said.

The man glanced at the package in her hand and she expected him to ask "What for?" When he didn't, she gave him another mark for good manners.

"He's over there, in the construction trailer," the man said, nodding in the direction she'd have to go. "Want me to get him for you?"

"That's okay," Roxie said quickly. "I'll find him. Thanks." She figured Hank would rather unwrap his valentine gift in private, anyway. If he had a refrigerator in the trailer, so much the better. Roxie was beginning to wonder if she'd had such a brilliant idea, after all. If Hank couldn't keep this thing in a cool place, he'd have the makings of a hot-fudge sundae minus the ice cream.

She skirted a pile of rolled insulation and walked toward the silver trailer with Craddock Construction and Design painted on the side in bold turquoise. She thought of the double responsibility that Hank carried running a business and raising two young children. He couldn't have a particularly easy life, and Roxie was glad she'd bought him something, no matter if it melted into a giant glob or not. He'd know that she'd tried.

She knocked on the half-open door of the trailer and Hank called to her to come in. After meeting him only once she recognized the distinctive timbre of his voice.

"Happy Valentine's Day," she said, pushing open the door and stepping inside the trailer.

"Roxie! What a neat surprise." As he stood up his smile of welcome creased his tanned cheeks and crinkled the corners of his eyes. He'd taken off the jacket he'd worn at her house, and the sleeves of his denim shirt were rolled back to his elbows.

Gazing at him standing behind a battered old desk amidst a cheerful clutter of plans, order receipts and Styrofoam coffee cups, Roxie wondered how she'd ever considered Doug, with his office pallor and carefully combed hair, attractive. "Your valentine message was great," she began, a little uncertainly. Charlie might believe that she and Hank were star-crossed lovers, but to Roxie he was still a semistranger. Intriguing, to be sure, but unknown.

"It was a pretty bad pun," he said. "Maybe I can blame it on my son. He got me started on that kick this morning when he gave me a homemade valentine that said 'To a guy who measures up.' It was a short jump from that to the pun about 'board.'"

"Your son made you a valentine? I think that's sweet."

"Yeah," he said softly. "They're good kids." He studied her for a moment. "I was touched that you included them in the invitation. Most of the women I know wouldn't have done that. They think Ryan and Hilary get in the way. And frankly, they do."

"Ryan and Hilary. Nice names." She felt guilty that he'd

praised her thoughtfulness. She hadn't invited his children out of consideration for them, but out of consideration for herself, to keep Hank at a safe distance until she was more certain of she wanted from this relationship. "I think they'll enjoy Como," she added lamely.

"I'm sure they will."

"Well, I—here," she said abruptly, placing the white box on his desk. "It's not homemade, but it's sort of symbolic, I guess. And unless you have a refrigerator in here, it won't last much longer."

"You brought me something?"

His look of delight stirred a tender place in her heart. Here was a man who had never lost the childlike anticipation of a surprise. "Open it carefully," she warned, "or you're liable to get messed up."

"Okay." He did as she instructed and slowly peeled back the lid. Then he glanced up at her with a grin. "Does this one work better than the one in my truck?"

Roxie laughed. "If it doesn't, I'll eat it."

"Oh, no, you don't. You're looking at a certified chocoholic. How did you know?"

"I didn't," she said, happier than she'd expected to be because she'd made a hit with her gift. "I guessed." Then she thought about Charlie's remarks about intuition. She wasn't surprised that Hank loved chocolate, but how could she have known it for certain?

"Well, this is great," Hank said. "Never in my life have I had a chocolate telephone. I had no idea such a thing existed."

"You don't know about that little shop near here? They mold chocolate into almost any shape imaginable."

"I've heard of the place but I never seem to have the time to go in. That's where this came from?"

"Yep. Chocolate freak that I am, I discovered that shop within a week of moving to Tucson."

Hank laughed. "I guess it takes a woman from New Jersey to point out some of the city's wonders to me. I'll bet there are all sorts of things I've missed around here."

She was so glad that he pronounced the name of her native state normally. "It's not your fault. You must be very busy."

"Sure, but I also believe in appreciating what's around you. If I've grown blasé about the great things in Tucson, maybe you can snap me out of my lethargy."

"The chocolate shop could be the only surprise I have."

He laughed. "Are you kidding? A gal who's llama-sitting and playing hostess to a character like Charlie Hartman? By the way, who is that guy, anyway? Your great-uncle or something?"

"Charlie is—" She paused and glanced at her watch. "Good grief. Speaking of Charlie, he must wonder what's keeping me. I told him I'd be right back and now we have less than half an hour before we have to leave for work. Besides, I've interrupted your schedule long enough."

"I don't mind," he said, his gray eyes telling her how very little he minded. "Where do you work?"

"County clerk's office."

"I've been there once."

"Not for any legal hassle, I hope."

"No. Marriage license. Of course, that was long before you started there."

"Yes." Roxie struggled with a negative emotion that she had no business feeling. She hardly knew Hank, and yet she resented the happy memory he must have of his one trip to the county clerk's office as a prospective bride-groom. "I'd really better go. I'll see you on Saturday, then."

"Okay." He smiled at her. "Thank you for the telephone.

I have a little refrigerator over there I can keep it in." He gestured toward a dusty corner filled with more rolled plans.

"That's good," she said, turning toward the door, "but promise me you'll eat it and not keep it around to look at. The chocolate is wonderful."

"I'll eat it, all right. I don't have the willpower not to. But I kind of hate to destroy the evidence."

She paused in her departure. "The evidence of what?"

"That you think our meeting this morning was as significant as I do. Happy Valentine's Day, Roxie."

She grinned at him. "Same to you." As she skipped down the trailer steps and hurried to her car, she felt like whistling. His last words had wiped out her silly jealousy about his wife and focused Roxie's attention on the present. Besides, a man who had loved well once was a proven quantity, wasn't he? Perhaps Charlie knew what he was doing, after all.

ROXIE HAD INVITED HANK and his children for five o'clock on Saturday, so that Ryan and Hilary could play with Como before dark. She'd debated the menu choice with Charlie all week—hamburgers to please the kids or her special chicken and mushroom dish to impress Hank? She'd finally settled on a compromise of pot roast—not too fancy and not too finicky, either. The scent of the cooking beef would welcome her guests when they arrived, and she wouldn't have to fuss with cooking while they were here.

Charlie was down in the guest house changing his shirt, and Roxie had just stepped out of the shower at four-thirty when Hank called.

"We may be a little late, Roxie," he apologized. "We've had a sort of...emergency here."

"My Lord, what? Is someone hurt?"

"No, no. Hilary—just a second, Roxie."

She heard murmurings on the other end, an energetic duet between Hank and one of his children, probably Hilary.

Finally Hank came back on the line. "I'm sorry, Roxie. My daughter has a problem which she doesn't want me to tell you about and she refuses to come tonight. I could drag her along anyway, but I'd rather not start the evening that way. I'll try to get a sitter and call you back."

Roxie twisted the telephone cord around her finger. "Is it...me? I've read that some little girls don't want their daddies to—"

"Whoa, whoa. Nothing like that. I've read those books, too, but that's not what we're dealing with here. It's much simpler than that. Hilary wanted to come to your house very much, so much in fact that she fixed herself up specially for the occasion."

Roxie heard childish protests in the background and Hank's assurances that he wouldn't tell what happened.

"Anyway," Hank said into the phone. "Her plan backfired a little, that's all."

"What if you can't get a sitter?"

"We'll cross that bridge when we come to it."

Roxie thought quickly. What had Hilary done to herself? Makeup could be washed off and outfits could be changed, so it must be her hair. She'd cut it or something. "Hank, could I talk with her for just a minute, if she'll let me?"

"I'll see." There was a long pause with more murmurings in the background.

Finally a small voice said "Hello?"

"Hi, Hilary. This is Roxie. I'm really sorry you can't come over and see Como, the llama."

"I can't because I look funny."

Roxie groped for the right words. "You know, Hilary,

when I was about seven I cut my own hair. I thought I could do a good job, but it wasn't such a good job when I finished."

There was a breathless pause. "What did you do then?"

Bingo, Roxie thought, *it's her hair*. "My mother tried to make it even, but she couldn't fix it all the way, so for a while I wore scarves. Do you have any pretty scarves?"

"I have one that used to be my mommy's," she said, a note of hope in her voice. "I play dress-up with it."

"There you go, Hilary. You could tie that scarf around your head and come over to play with Como. Then your brother won't have all the fun."

There was silence on the other end while Hilary thought about the suggestion. "Okay," she said at last, "if I can keep that scarf on every minute."

"Sure you can. I'll see you soon, then."

"Okay. Bye."

Roxie laughed when Hilary hung up the phone without bothering to find out if her father wanted to say anything more. When he didn't call her back Roxie figured they were on their way and she hurried through the rest of her dressing routine.

By the time she returned to the kitchen and began preparing the salad, Charlie was walking across the patio toward the back door. His step was spry, she thought, for someone who must be at least seventy-five. He'd never been willing to discuss his exact age except to say that he'd seen "too many winters for her to count them all."

She thought again of Charlie's vulnerable position and what would happen to him if he lost his robust health. Somehow, she decided, she would watch out for him, even if it meant scrimping a little on her own needs. Charlie was becoming like family to her.

"My, but you look wonderful," Charlie exclaimed as he

came through the French doors into the kitchen. "That sea-green sweater and slacks outfit is the perfect complement to your eyes and hair."

"Thank you, Charlie." She appreciated his comments. She wanted to look good tonight. Poor little Hilary had wanted to look good, too, and Roxie's heart went out to her. Maybe, if the evening went well, Hilary would let her take out the scissors and repair some of the damage. "We almost didn't have guests. I talked to Hank about twenty minutes ago and his daughter didn't want to come. I think she tried to cut her own hair and she was embarrassed to have us see her that way."

"But they are coming?" Charlie looked anxious.

"Yes. I talked Hilary into it. I told her to wear a pretty scarf."

"Excellent." Charlie rubbed his hands and smiled at her. "Did you use logic or intuition in this case?"

"A little of both, I suppose," Roxie admitted, putting the bowl of salad in the refrigerator. She glanced at him. "Don't worry, Charlie. You're having an effect on me."

"Nonsense. You've always had an intuitive side. You merely have to listen to discover it."

The doorbell rang and they glanced at each other.

Roxie fluffed her hair and took a deep breath. "What does your intuition tell you about tonight, Charlie?"

"I think one of your space-age expressions would fit in this case." Charlie gave his gold pin a quick swipe with his handkerchief.

"Which one?" she asked as they walked toward the front door together.

"All systems go."

4

THE FAMILY PORTRAIT that greeted Roxie when she opened the heavy carved door was incomplete. She could almost see a dotted line drawn around the spot where Hank's wife should have been. Here stood the handsome, square-jawed father holding the hand of a little girl with a blue and lavender scarf tied over her brown hair. Next to them, close enough for security but far enough to establish his growing independence, was the blond, hesitant son. They had arranged themselves as if making room for someone else who had once turned the odd number to even.

Roxie felt the tug, the urge to fill that gaping hole herself, and knew that she couldn't be the only woman to have felt that way. She'd have to be careful, very careful, not to let that emotion influence her attraction to Hank. She had to like him for himself, not his needy situation. He might not see himself as needy, anyway. Perhaps he imagined that everything was fine with this little family unit. But she could tell at a glance that it wasn't.

"I'm so glad you all made it," she said, smiling at Hilary in particular. "Come in and meet Charlie Hartman, a dear friend of mine."

"And these are my children, Ryan and Hilary," Hank said with obvious pride. "Kids, this is Roxie Lowell, the lady who gave me the chocolate telephone."

Hilary fiddled with the buttons on her coat. "We ate the receiver already," she volunteered. "I didn't want to, but those guys said we couldn't keep the chocolate forever. I don't like eating things with shapes."

"Hilary!" Ryan whispered and nudged his sister with his elbow. "That's not nice." He glanced around the room with polite, grown-up interest. "I see that you have a wide-screen TV."

"The Osborns do, the people I'm taking care of the house for," Roxie said.

"Ryan's trying to change the subject," Hilary said with a wise little look. "But it's true. I don't like eating shapes."

"I understand," Roxie said, smiling at her. The little girl had doused herself with perfume for the occasion, perhaps to distract everyone from her problem with her hair. "At least the chocolate wasn't in the shape of an animal, though."

"Boy, that would have been terrible," Hilary agreed. "Once I got a chocolate rabbit for Easter and everybody wanted me to eat it. Ryan—" she paused to glare at her brother "—told me to bite the head right off. But I wouldn't."

"Good girl," Charlie said, nodding in approval.

"Yeah, and the rabbit melted in her closet," Ryan added with disgust. "Mom found it on the Fourth of July. In her bunny slippers."

Roxie felt another pang of regret for this threesome. It would have been a funny story, if their mother had been there to tell it. "Well!" she began, rubbing her hands briskly. "Speaking of animals, would you like to go straight out to the patio and see the llama before you take off your coats?"

"I would," Hilary said right away.

"Sure," Ryan added, but more casually. He was in training for adolescence, Roxie could see, and didn't want to appear childishly eager for anything.

Charlie stepped forward on cue. "I'll take them, Roxie, while you finish up the dinner preparations."

"Okay, thanks." Roxie still had gravy to make and a few last touches to give the table setting.

"I'll stay and help Roxie," Hank said. "After all, I've already met Como. You kids go on out with Charlie."

As simply as that, Roxie thought, as if they were in cahoots, Charlie and Hank had arranged things so that the valentine couple would be alone for a while. She didn't mind, though. A little time to themselves, without the danger of an entire evening stretching before them, would be nice.

"I like llamas," Hilary said, exchanging her father's hand for Charlie's as if she'd known him for years. "I petted one once at the zoo. They're soft."

"I think Como will like both of you, too," Charlie said, leading Hilary away with Ryan following close behind.

Roxie watched them go and tried to imagine what sort of damage Hilary's scarf was hiding. Her brown bangs looked okay, so she must have hacked off part of the back. That was good. Bangs were harder to fix than the sides and back of a haircut.

"The scarf idea was a brainstorm. Thanks," Hank said. "I hope you don't mind if she eats her dinner with it on. She made me promise that she could."

Roxie looked fully into his gray eyes for the first time since he and his children had arrived. Probing the emotions reflected in them was like tasting a rich dessert, she thought. She wanted more, but doubted that her system could handle it. "Hilary can eat dinner wrapped in a sheet if she likes, although I was hoping that later on I'd win her confidence enough that she'd let me look at the damage. Maybe I could do something."

He chuckled. "I doubt it."

"You never know. I'm handy with scissors. Maybe I could even out the places where she's cut it."

"That's not the problem, and we'd better stop talking about it or I'll tell you the whole story, and I swore to her that I wouldn't."

Roxie laughed. "Now I'm dying to know what she's done, but you're a nice daddy to keep your word. I won't pester you about it."

"Thanks. She'd be furious if I spilled the beans, and I'd pay the consequences for a long time. Hilary has a memory like an elephant and she doesn't forgive easily."

Roxie nodded in understanding. "I'm kind of like that, myself. That's why when I thought you were married, I—well, never mind. Since you're not going out to see Como, why don't I take your jacket?"

"Fine." He shrugged out of the jacket and handed it to her. "I...take it you had a bad experience with someone?"

"Yes. But let's not go into that subject right now, either." She hung his jacket in the closet and ran her fingers lightly down the supple suede. The color reminded her of toasted muffins—a natural color that suited a man like Hank. She turned and noticed that he'd worn khaki slacks and a soft brown shirt open at the collar. She had the inappropriate desire to knead his shoulders as she would warm earth, and kiss him hello. Instead she offered him a drink.

"I'll take bourbon if you've got it," he said, "but only one before dinner, since I'm the chauffeur tonight."

"You'll probably laugh at this, but I keep my liquor supply in the kitchen. The Osborns have a perfectly good wet bar in the recreation room, but I hate to spot up the stainless steel sink for a drink or two and I don't give parties."

"Sounds logical to me."

Roxie gave him a rueful glance. "I've been told I favor that trait a little too much. Anyway, if we have our drinks in the kitchen I can finish my work and you can peek out the window to see how the kids and Charlie are getting along."

"Makes sense," he said, following her toward the back of the house, "although I'm sure the kids and Charlie are doing just fine. I've never seen Hilary take a stranger's hand that quickly before."

"He has a way with people," Roxie said as she opened the cupboard and took out the bourbon. "He won my heart in about five minutes."

"You say that as if you haven't known him very long. Did he come with the house or something, like the llama?"

Roxie was extremely aware of Hank as he leaned against the counter, but somehow she maintained her poise while he watched her make the drinks. "I don't know how you'll react to my story about Charlie," she said. "I met him my first day on the job." She paused to take the ice-cube tray out of the freezer.

"Here, I'll do that." Hank took the plastic tray and with one quick twist loosened the cubes and dumped them in the ice bucket. Roxie had forgotten how nice it was to have an adept man around. Charlie tried, but conveniences such as plastic ice trays and electric dishwashers baffled him.

"So Charlie works down at the county clerk's office?" Hank asked.

"No, but he comes in every day." She put ice in the glasses and started to pour the bourbon. "How strong?"

"Weak."

She sloshed less than a jigger of bourbon in each glass and took the cold water from the refrigerator to fill them to the top. When she started to hand one glass to Hank she drew it back abruptly. "This is stupid," she said, shaking her head. "I made this without asking you how you liked your bourbon. I can start over if you want Seven-up or something else with it."

"I like it exactly like this." Hank took the glass and waited for Roxie to pick up hers. "Follow your intuition where I'm concerned and you'll probably be right on target."

"What did you say?" She glanced at him in surprise.

"I'm not tough to figure out. I'm a pretty transparent guy."

"No, that's not what you said. You mentioned something about intuition."

"Well, yeah, I guess I did." He grinned at her. "The fact is that I do operate on intuition a lot. And a few minutes ago you were emphasizing how logical you are."

"I *am* logical, Hank."

"Then why didn't you ask me how I liked my bourbon?"

She stared at him for several seconds. "I don't know."

"Intuition?"

She conceded the point with a smile. Logic hadn't governed anything she'd done concerning Hank Craddock, yet his presence here felt exactly right. The pleasure of being with him tonight reminded her of the moments as a child when she'd curled up in a sunny window seat with a book she'd been wanting to read for a long time. "My intuition also tells me that I'm going to like you very much," she admitted.

He gazed at her. "Mine tells me the same about you." He touched the rim of his glass to hers. "Here's to our intuition."

She acknowledged the toast with a nod and sipped her bourbon.

"I guess you have work to do, huh?"

"Yes," she said, reluctantly moving out of the magic circle that surrounded them. "Gravy."

"Can I help?"

"Gravy's a one-person job," she said, rummaging for pot holders, "but you're welcome to keep me company while I work."

"My pleasure. There's nothing nicer than a warm kitchen and the smell of good food." He paused. "Well, almost nothing, anyway."

Her stomach lurched at his implication and she made herself very busy taking the roast out of the oven and finding a platter for it. "How're the kids doing?" she said in an effort to appear nonchalant and in control.

"Great. Ryan's leading Como, and Hilary's riding her. They look like they're having a ball."

"Good." Roxie took the roast out and put it on a platter.

"You still haven't told me who Charlie is."

As she covered the meat with tinfoil she wondered how to describe Charlie's situation, but she couldn't come up with any way to gild the lily. "He's a bum," she said finally.

"What?"

"I'm not joking, Hank." She turned to him. "Before I brought him to live in the guest house the night it snowed, he was living on a park bench downtown. Haven't you noticed that his clothes are somewhat frayed?"

"Well, sure, but sometimes old people become attached to certain clothes and wear them to shreds." He laughed. "Not just old people. I have a pair of jeans with holes everywhere and I wouldn't dream of parting with them." He gazed at her. "He really lived in the park?"

"Yep." Roxie paused to sip from the drink she'd placed nearby on the counter. "And when the snow came I was afraid he'd freeze to death on that bench, so I invited him to stay in the Osborns' guest house. Turns out we get along very well, and he's been here ever since."

"Well, I'll be damned. What do you know about him?" Hank glanced out the kitchen window again.

"Not a whole lot, if you mean cold, hard facts," Roxie said, noticing the direction of his glance. "But he wouldn't hurt a flea, Hank. The children are safe with him. I'd stake my life on it."

"I tend to believe you, especially with the way Hilary and Ryan seem to be having such a good time out there. And Como likes him, too. It's hard to distrust someone who attracts children and animals."

"And is such a romantic," Roxie added. "I met Charlie that first day at work, when he brought in a red rose."

"He did what?"

"Every weekday morning, since about the time I started working there, I guess, he's brought a red rose for the bud vase on the counter of the clerk's office. He says they're for the couples taking out marriage licenses."

Hank swirled the ice cubes in his drink. "That's pretty amazing in itself. Where does he get the money for the rose, if he's broke?"

"No one's had the nerve to ask him, including me. I suppose if he stays here long enough I'll find out if he picks up a public assistance check every month or something."

"Could he be, ah, appropriating the roses from somewhere?"

Roxie shook her head. "Not Charlie. I've believed in his honesty ever since I met him, which is ironic considering how illogical that is. There's another area where I suppose I've let intuition take over, so maybe I'm not as logical as I think."

"Maybe not." Hank looked pleased with the idea. "I'll sure never forget the first day *I* met him. Here he came, an old English-looking gentleman leading a llama. I thought I had some resident who hadn't bothered to complain about the construction before but was ready to burn my behind about it now. Instead he complimented me on the job and implied that my name had something to do with it."

"I know." Returning to her task, she used a slotted spoon to dish the carrots and potatoes into a stoneware bowl before returning them to the warm oven. "He commented on your name the first time he saw it on the sign. He's very big on this meaning of names thing."

"Then he must have told you what yours means."

Roxie got out the flour for the gravy without looking at him. "Yes, he did."

"And what did he say?"

"It's all pretty silly, don't you think?" Roxie stirred a mixture of flour and water into the drippings from the pot roast.

"Probably, but I'm still curious, now that we're on the subject."

"Okay." Roxie stirred vigorously, scraping the metal spoon in rapid circles around the bottom of the Dutch oven. "He said that Lowell means 'beloved,'" she mumbled.

"What? I couldn't hear you."

"Beloved," she repeated in a louder voice.

"Hmm."

The back of Roxie's neck grew warm. She knew he was staring at her and she was afraid to turn around and catch him at it.

"What do you make of that?" His voice was closer.

"Nothing." She kept stirring as if the atmosphere of the room hadn't changed, as if she weren't holding her breath in anticipation of his next words.

"It seems a strange coincidence that according to Charlie my name means *abounding in love* and yours means *beloved*."

"Yes, but I'm sure it's only a coincidence." She was sure it wasn't.

"*Beloved*." Hank repeated, as if he liked saying it. "That sounds good. It suits you, Roxie. Tell me, what does Charlie think will happen if two people with names like ours meet on St. Valentine's Day?"

From the corner of her eye she could see that he was right beside her now. Summoning her courage, she glanced up at him. "Oh, as you can imagine, he thinks we're destined for each other." She tried to laugh, as if it was a joke, but the laugh stuck in her throat.

"That's interesting."

"It's...crazy, of course," she murmured, unable to unfasten her gaze from his. Her stirring of the gravy became slower and slower.

He took a deep breath and put down his drink. "I wish that I'd known you a little longer, Roxie."

"Why?" she whispered.

"Because I'm going to kiss you, and Charlie or no Charlie, you'll probably think I have no business doing that yet."

The spoon slipped from her trembling fingers and landed with a plop in the gravy. "I...don't know what to think, about any of this."

"Don't worry. Neither do I." Gently he turned her toward him. "Except that I've wanted to touch you ever since the moment we met." He cradled the curve of her jaw in his hand and tipped her face up to his.

Tentatively she laid her hands against his chest. His warmth welcomed her chilled fingers as she had imagined it would. "I've thought about touching you, too," she confessed, and watched his eyes as she increased the pressure of her hands and moved up to his shoulders. The effect was as if she'd struck a match with the friction. "But I kept telling myself that we barely know each other."

"That's not the way it feels, though, is it?"

She shook her head.

"We'll be okay," he murmured, closing the distance between them.

Heart pounding, Roxie closed her eyes and waited for the first sweet pressure of his lips. She felt the whisper touch of his breath and smelled the tang of bourbon. She wound her arms around his neck. Just as his lips grazed hers, a screech from the backyard wedged between them and they reeled away from each other in shock. After one startled glance at each other they raced for the French doors into the patio and almost collided with Hilary.

"My scarf came off," she wailed, pushing past them and racing through the kitchen in a frantic search for privacy. "Don't look!"

"Hilary," her father said, his tone stern. "Come back and let us—"

"I can't!" she cried and charged down the hall and into the first room she found. Immediately she closed the door.

"Young lady, you can't just—" Hank started after her.

"Wait." Roxie caught his arm. "She's in my room, and she won't hurt anything in there. Let her regain her dignity."

Charlie and Ryan came through the French doors discussing the incident between them.

"It wasn't my fault," Ryan said.

"Of course not," Charlie agreed. "You couldn't have known that Como would try to nibble on that scarf."

"And it wasn't your fault, either," Ryan continued loyally.

"No, these things happen, don't they?" Charlie said, patting Ryan on the back. "And it certainly wasn't Como's fault. She didn't understand how important that scarf was to Hilary's well-being."

Roxie glanced at them and chuckled. "Have you two absolved everyone of blame?"

Charlie looked worried. "I did so want everything to go smoothly. Is she terribly upset?"

"Well..."

"She is," Charlie said, wringing his hands. "Of course she is, poor child. Anyone with spotted hair would be upset."

"I know," Ryan suggested. "We'll all pretend we didn't see her spotted hair because she was running so fast."

Hank gave Ryan an appreciative look. "That's nice of you to think of Hilary's feelings, but I doubt if she'll believe us. I think she's well aware that her secret's out."

"What *did* happen?" Roxie asked. "Did she try to bleach her hair?"

"I told her it was a dumb idea," Ryan said, taking off his jacket. "I had to ride my bike over to the shopping center and buy the junk, 'cause she's not allowed to ride there yet."

"Hilary offered Ryan a sizable tip," Hank added, "and since then Ryan and I have talked about whether to go along with such plans in the future."

"I sure wouldn't have," Ryan insisted, "if I'd known she'd make such a mess. Plus that stuff really stinks. She smelled up our bathroom something awful, and she stinks, too. That's why she put on all that perfume."

The subject of smells made Roxie aware of a scorched scent that was invading their area. "The gravy!" she cried and dashed to the stove. What had begun as smooth brown gravy had become a leathery substance pasted to the bottom of the pan.

Hank came over to the stove. "Oh, well," he remarked,

surveying the damage. "We can do without gravy." He glanced sideways at her. "Sorry about that."

She gazed back at him and remembered what had almost been a memorable moment. "All things considered, it doesn't matter."

"No." There was a definite caress in his tone.

Roxie stood smiling at him until she remembered that they had an audience. She looked over her shoulder and found both Charlie and Ryan watching them with interest, too much interest for her tastes. "How would you guys like to finish setting the table for me?" she asked and moved away from Hank. "The napkins and napkin rings are in the top drawer of the buffet in the dining room. Then we'll need butter, and the salt and pepper shakers aren't on yet. Oh, and milk for Ryan and Hilary and ice water for the rest of us. I'll make coffee later."

"Come along, Ryan, old chap," Charlie said, putting his arm around Ryan's shoulder and leading him toward the dining room. "We've been pressed into service."

"Wow," Hank said when they'd left. "I didn't realize that you had such marshalling skills."

"I keep telling you that I'm logical, which makes me a great organizer."

"Mmm," he murmured, teasing her with a glance. "Then what happened to the gravy?"

"I was distracted."

"I see. Upset?"

"No," she said softly, "but now it's time to get this show on the road. I did offer to feed your family, and Ryan looks starved."

"Ryan is always starved. But I guess you're right—we should tend to the troops." He sighed. "Unfortunately. Next time I'd better plan better."

Roxie's stomach churned as she imagined a next time

with Hank, without interruptions. As a flush rose to her cheeks she quickly opened the refrigerator and took out the salad and dressing. "Here. You can toss this while I talk to Hilary."

"You don't have to do that," Hank said, taking the large wooden bowl and a bottle of dressing from her. "She'll probably be much happier if we leave her alone in your room until it's time to go."

"Maybe, but I'd like to try convincing her to come out. That is, if it's okay."

"Sure, go ahead. But I can't guarantee she'll be all sweetness and light."

Roxie chuckled. "Can you ever guarantee that about a kid? I had my moments when I was that age."

"I just bet you did." His gray gaze swept over her. "I wish I could have been there."

"But then we wouldn't be here, would we?" she pointed out.

"God, you are logical, aren't you?"

"Uh-huh. Now toss the salad, and hope that I'll be back soon with Hilary."

"I hope you'll be back soon, period."

She knew from the light in his eyes that he meant it. "Thank you."

"You're welcome. Listen, Roxie, there's something you should know. She wants to bleach her hair so she'll be a blond like her mother was."

"Oh." Roxie felt strange having Hank mention his wife so soon after he'd admitted his attraction to someone else. She thought of the blond woman in the photograph that she'd seen so briefly Tuesday morning. "I can understand that," she said, proud of herself for sounding so calm about the subject. "Your wife was very beautiful."

"Yes, she was."

It hurt Roxie to hear him admit that, but what else could she expect him to say? *Well, she was okay, but nothing compared to you?* Roxie wouldn't have liked him much for saying something like that about a woman he'd loved, anyway. For the moment Roxie was glad that she was a small-boned redhead, though. At least Hank couldn't be trying to replace his blond, Scandinavian-looking wife with her. "I'll see what I can do about Hilary," she said.

"Thanks."

She walked down the hall and knocked at her own bedroom door, which seemed an odd thing to be doing.

"Who is it?" Hilary said, sounding as if she had her lips right up against the door.

The poor girl must have been trying to listen to the conversation in the other part of the house, Roxie thought. Of course Hilary would know that they'd been talking about her and her abortive attempt to bleach her hair. Fortunately the walls were thick and the heater ducts didn't run from Roxie's room to the kitchen.

"It's Roxie," she said. "May I come in?"

"Is this your room?"

"Yes, but you don't have to let me in unless you want to."

"I thought it was your room," Hilary said, her voice muffled through the door. "It smells like you."

Roxie smiled. "I hope that's good."

"It's good. You smell lots better than I do, that's for sure." She sounded miserable.

"Hilary, I'd like to talk to you about fixing your hair."

"Daddy says it can't be fixed. He says it'll have to grow out. That might not be until I'm in the fourth grade. I think I'll probably quit school until then."

She sounded so serious that Roxie had to cover her mouth to keep from laughing. This was serious to Hilary, and would have been to her when she was eight. "Hilary, daddies are wonderful people, but they don't know everything about hair. I don't think you'll have to wait for it to grow out."

"I won't?" Hope raised the pitch of her voice.

"I don't think so. Will you let me take a look?"

"Okay." Hilary opened the door. She'd taken off her coat, and she looked like a little immigrant in her red and white dress and her mother's lavender and blue scarf tied under her chin.

"Let's sit on my bed and talk," Roxie suggested, taking her hand and leading her back into the room.

"Okay," Hilary said again. "Want to see my hair?" Now that a solution was in sight, she seemed eager to show Roxie the damage.

"Yes, I do." Roxie waited for the unveiling and winced when Hilary removed the scarf. Her hair was at least four different colors ranging from a strange orange to brunette in uneven splotches over her medium-length hair. The cut, a modified pageboy with very little curl, did nothing to disguise the odd color combination.

"Well?" Hilary turned a worried gaze toward Roxie.

"I think maybe it can be fixed," Roxie proclaimed and prayed that she was right. "A woman I know who works in a beauty shop should be able to cover the bleached parts well enough so it won't be so noticeable."

"Oh, no!" Hilary said, her gray eyes widening in dismay. "I want them to bleach the *rest* of it. I don't want to be a brown-head anymore. That's why I did this in the first place. I don't want anybody to dye it *back*."

"Ah." Roxie began to take in the scope of the problem. Reversing Hilary's experiment back to brown would be expensive, but Roxie figured Hank would agree to pay to restore peace to his household and assure that Hilary would finish the third grade. He didn't look like the kind of man who would approve of his daughter becoming a blond bombshell at the age of eight.

"Can the beauty shop do that, bleach all of my hair the same color?" Hilary persisted.

Roxie hesitated. This was rocky terrain. "I think so, but it takes a long time, hours. You have to sit very still, and if the stuff gets on your skin, it stings, according to a friend of mine. I don't think you'd like going through all of that."

"Yes, I would." Hilary folded her arms across her chest and stuck out her chin. "I would sit there for two days if I had to."

"Hilary, your real color is very pretty," Roxie said, although she doubted her words would have much effect.

"You sound just like Daddy," Hilary said in disgust. "He doesn't understand anything. Brown hair looks good on him but not on me."

"Well, I'll tell you what." Roxie wondered if she was about to make a tremendous mistake to get involved with this problem.

"What?" Instantly Hilary was eager again. She obviously viewed Roxie as her only hope of salvation.

"I'll talk to your daddy about this."

Hilary looked pleased with that idea. "Can you tell him I'll be much prettier if my hair is blond?"

"No, because I can't imagine that you'll be prettier."

"Oh, yes, I will," the little girl asserted solemnly.

"But I'll tell him that something needs to be done. I wouldn't want to go to school like that, either. Now how about some dinner?"

"Well, I am kind of hungry," Hilary admitted. She looked up at Roxie. "I really do want to be a blonde."

"I know, sweetheart." Roxie hugged her. "I'll talk it over

with your daddy later. Right now I think we should eat, though, don't you?"

"I guess so. Do you think I should wear my scarf?"

"Not unless you want to."

"It feels funny and I might drip something on it."

"Then why not leave it off? We're all friends here."

Hilary scowled. "Except Ryan. He'd better not call me a punk rocker."

"We'll tell him not to," Roxie said, standing.

"Yeah." Hilary jumped off the bed and walked toward Roxie's dresser. "Did my daddy give you this?" She held up the piece of two-by-four with Hank's writing on it.

"Yes, as a joke." Roxie didn't want Hilary making too much of the impromptu valentine.

"He likes you, huh?"

Roxie met Hilary's wide, innocent gaze. "I think so. Is that okay?"

"It's okay," Hilary said, replacing the wood on the dresser.

Roxie felt as if she'd passed some sort of test, and she sighed with relief. "Do you like chocolate cake?" she asked, certain of the answer.

"I don't like chocolate cake," Hilary corrected. "I *love* it."

"Then we'd better start on dinner so you can have some for dessert."

"Chocolate cake! Yum!" Hilary grabbed Roxie's hand and pulled her down the hall. "Let's go!" She practically ran into Hank.

"I was coming to see if you two fell in," he said.

Hilary gazed up at her father. "We were talking," she said. "Later Roxie's going to talk to you about bleaching my hair. I want to find my place at the table. Bye." She dashed down the hall, her multicolored hair flying behind her.

Roxie gulped. "Hank, I—"

"Never mind," he said, laying his hand on her arm. "We can talk about it later. I'm determined to make time for us to be alone, anyway. We have some unfinished business to attend to."

5

CHARLIE ENTERTAINED everyone at dinner with stories about exotic people and places. Even Roxie was impressed when Charlie mentioned having met the Duke and Duchess of Windsor at a reception in New York City years ago, and Clark Gable and Carole Lombard during a gala reception for them in Hollywood. The stories distracted Roxie from Hank's promise of time to be alone, but every once in a while she'd catch him gazing at her and be reminded of the kiss that almost happened.

If they hadn't been interrupted, she would have kissed Hank without having time to think about it. The cozy warmth of the kitchen and the relaxing effects of the bourbon had given her a sense of well-being, but as the evening continued she'd grown anxious about Hank's intentions.

At first she couldn't figure out why she was nervous about a simple kiss and a few stolen moments alone. She'd shared that much with Doug Kelly without this stomach-tightening worry. Finally she identified the difference. She'd never been in danger of losing her heart to Doug, but Hank was a different story.

Hank had aroused emotions that threatened to make her vulnerable again. When she'd left New Jersey and the man who had betrayed her, she'd been fragile as a soap bubble. Rebuilding her confidence had taken most of her energy for six months, and she'd vowed not to open her heart again so easily. Yet for a moment in Hank's arms she'd abandoned her caution.

At least for now she was protected from her own weaknesses by Charlie and Hank's children, who wouldn't be going outside again now that it was dark. Perhaps she had nothing more to worry about tonight and she could evaluate the situation in the morning, without Hank's presence to muddle her thinking. She began to relax until Ryan unknowingly jerked away her safety net.

"Does that wide-screen TV have a VCR with it?" he asked as he scraped the last of his second piece of chocolate cake from his plate.

"Yes," Roxie replied, "but we don't have much in the way of video tapes for it."

"No movies?"

"Just some travel films the Osborns made during their trips to Europe and Africa. I've seen them and they're a little boring, to tell the truth."

"I've never watched a movie on a wide-screen TV before," Ryan continued, broadening his hint. "Some kids told me it's almost like being at the show."

Hank cleared his throat. "I think Ryan's suggesting in his not-so-subtle manner that he'd like us to rent a movie to top off the evening."

"Yeah!" Ryan beamed. "That would be great."

"Well, I guess we could do that," Roxie said. "Would everyone else like to?"

"I would," Hilary announced. "We could get *Old Yeller*."

"Naw," Ryan said. "Something with action, like *Top Gun*."

"I won't have any arguments," Hank began, folding his napkin beside his plate, "but if you two promise to be satisfied with what we choose, Roxie and I will pick up a movie for you."

Roxie paused with her fork in midair. Hank had arranged for them to be alone and she hadn't even seen it coming. "Why don't you and Charlie go while I clean up?" she said quickly.

Charlie shook his head. "Roxie, my dear, you know that I'm not up on the latest films. I'd be of no use, not to mention the fact that you shouldn't clean the kitchen after all your work on the meal. While you're gone, the children and I will do the dishes."

"But—" Roxie's protestations were starting to look silly and she knew it. "Okay. Thanks," she said and glanced at Hank, who was looking very puzzled by her reaction. And why shouldn't he? Earlier in the evening she'd given him every indication that she wanted what he wanted. In some ways, she did.

"So run along, you two," Charlie said, waving his hand. "Take your time."

Roxie stood as Hank pulled back her chair for her. "Just clearing the table would be plenty," she suggested. "Don't bother with the dishwasher." She remembered Charlie's bewilderment with pop-open measuring cups and rinse cycles.

"Now, now," Charlie said, rising from the table. "Don't worry about us. I have a capable cleanup crew here, haven't I?" He raised his shaggy white eyebrows and peered at Ryan and Hilary.

"Sure," Ryan said, proud of his abilities. "I run the dishwasher at home all the time."

"Don't trouble yourselves," Roxie said again. "Just clearing would be a big help."

"We'll see, we'll see," Charlie said, ushering them both toward the coat closet. "You take your time, now."

Roxie glanced at the old man. He knew exactly what was going on and was delighted with the outcome of his scheming. She hadn't really minded his game of matchmaking until now, until she'd begun to understand the risk involved.

"Any of the *Star Trek* movies, Dad," Ryan called after them. "Or maybe Chuck Norris."

"No," Hilary protested. "*Old Yeller*, Daddy."

"We'll see what we can find," Hank said as he helped Roxie on with her coat. "Remember that anything we rent will be a treat, and I don't want complaining about which movie we bring back, okay?"

"Okay," the kids said together, although they glared at each other afterward.

"Kids..." Hank said under his breath as he opened the front door and they stepped into the crisp February night. "It's a constant challenge, isn't it?"

"You're doing beautifully with them," Roxie said, thankfully grasping at the topic of his children as they headed for the charged privacy of his gray Lincoln Continental. "And speaking of that, I don't want to interfere in this business of Hilary's hair, but I promised her I'd talk with you about it. There might be an alternative to letting it grow out."

He opened the passenger door. "Like what?"

"A good hairdresser might be able to even up the color a little and make it less startling."

"I'd be willing to consider that, I guess," Hank said, looking at her. "My first angry reaction was to let her live with it."

"I understand, but I think she's suffered the consequences quite a bit already." Roxie sailed happily into her debate mode. She might make it through this drive if they could maintain a heated discussion about Hilary. "Of course, what she really wants is for someone to dye it blond."

Hank didn't answer until he was around the car and behind the wheel. "I tell you frankly I'm not in favor of that."

"I'm not, either. I had an idea, but there's an element of risk. What if you told her she could be blond, but first she had to watch the whole process being done on someone else?" Roxie asked as he started the car. "I can't believe she'd still want to go through with it after about three hours of watching someone else have it done."

"And what if she still does?" Hank pulled out of the drive.

"There's your element of risk. But Hank, unless she gives up this idea of her own accord, she's liable to hang on to this belief that she has to be blond to be pretty."

"She's a beautiful little girl!" Hank said in a frustrated tone. "Surely she knows that. I tell her all the time."

Roxie sighed. "You're her father, the guy who's supposed to say that. She doesn't really believe you, especially when she knows that you don't want her to bleach her hair."

"She's right about that."

"I realize that I have no room to talk, because I don't have children," Roxie said, thinking she'd better concede that particular point before Hank used it against her, "but I think she needs to be the one who decides not to be a blonde."

He glanced at her and smiled. "Considering that I'm getting this advice from logical, practical Roxie, perhaps I ought to listen. Let me think about it."

Roxie was stunned. He was giving up that easily? "On the other hand, perhaps a haircut would take care of the damage without risking the chance that she'll choose the dye job."

"Whatever you think. I've just about decided that you

should handle this, if you'd consider taking her to the beauty shop."

"Oh, no, I—she's your daughter, and I don't want to talk you into anything that might—"

"Isn't that what you've been trying to do with all those careful arguments?"

She looked over at him and discovered that he was smiling. "I—I guess so."

"Then you win. Simple as that. In fact, I appreciate your sharing the load on this crisis. It's lonely at the top."

She was silent for a few moments. He was affecting her emotions again. No matter how much she tried, she couldn't turn off her compassion for his situation. And she liked him, dammit. He was a fair and understanding man, an easy person to be around. Too easy. She searched for another conversational distraction. "Somehow I expected we'd be riding in your truck," she said.

"I wish we were. It has a bench seat," he replied reaching for her hand, "but the kids like this car. The radio's better."

She panicked. He was moving right along on schedule. She could take her hand away but then they'd have to talk about that, and she didn't want to. "Does this car have a telephone, like the truck does?" Maybe she could call the house on the pretext of checking on the kids and Charlie. It wasn't really a pretext; she wasn't very confident about what might be going on there.

"No telephone." He glanced at her, and the dim light made his face seem more rugged and mysterious than ever before. "Is there someone you wanted to call?"

"I just thought maybe we should make sure everything's okay with the cleanup operation."

"Ah." He released her hand. "What is it, Roxie?" he asked softly. "What's the matter? You tried to get out of taking this drive, and then you wanted to discuss Hilary forever. Now you're suggesting we call home.''

She laughed nervously. What could she say, that he was exactly the sort of man she could love, and she was afraid to let that happen because she was still healing from her last episode? No. Something more vague. ''I don't know. One minute it seems as if I've known you forever, and the next I wonder how I can be so attracted to someone I met for the first time four days ago.''

''But you are attracted?'' he said with a smile, and retrieved her hand. ''Your fingers are icy cold. Are you really that nervous?''

''I don't know what you have in mind.'' That was closer to the truth than she'd intended.

''You mean tonight, or long-term?''

She wanted an answer to both, foolish as that sounded even to her. ''Tonight, of course,'' she said in her most logical tone. ''After all, we've just met.''

''What about Charlie's prediction? Don't you have any faith in that?''

''Not...not really.''

''I see. Well, then, I'll tell you what I have in mind for tonight. No tricks. We'll pick up a movie, probably a comedy or something that neither of the kids asked for specifically, but they'll be happy with. Then we'll stop on a quiet side street and find out how the end of that kiss goes.''

She wondered if he could hear her heart thundering in the close confines of the car.

''Any objections so far?''

''I...no, I guess not.'' She swallowed. ''And then?''

He glanced at her and smiled. ''If we both like it a lot, we'll have to make a date, without the kids, so that we can explore the possibilities further. We did promise to bring home a movie sometime this evening, and I can't let Ryan down after he gave me exactly the opening I needed to have a moment alone with you."

"Hank, maybe with the kids waiting and everything, we should pick up the movie and go straight home. Doesn't that make more sense?"

He rubbed his thumb against her palm. "Maybe, but then I wouldn't get to kiss you tonight. I don't want to go home without knowing what your lips feel like, Roxie. I could do it, but I don't want to."

His words built an excitement in her that shouted down her caution. She could chance a kiss, couldn't she? One kiss didn't mean surrendering her life to him.

Hank turned into the shopping center parking lot and parked in front of the video store. "Are you with me on this?" he asked, swiveling toward her. "If you want to choose the movie and go straight home, we'll do that."

She gazed at him and knew this was a crossroads that she'd remember forever. "I don't want to go straight home."

"Good." He traced her jawline with his finger. "Neither do I. Now let's find a movie, fast."

They toured the aisles quickly, hand in hand. After a few minutes Hank took a family comedy from the shelf and led Roxie back to the checkout counter. "This'll do," he said, reaching in his back pocket for his wallet.

As they left the brightness of the video store for the hushed calm of the Lincoln's interior, Roxie could think of nothing more to say. Hank, too, was silent as he tossed the movie in the back seat and wheeled the Lincoln out of the parking lot.

A short distance later Hank swerved the car into the vacant cul-de-sac of a new housing development and cut the engine. "I feel about sixteen," he murmured, unfastening his seat belt and turning toward her. "I guess stolen kisses in the car aren't really my style anymore."

She unfastened her own belt and faced him. "Was it ever anybody's style?" she said gently.

"No. Especially not with these seats and a console in between. We're getting out." Before she could reply he'd left his seat and was rounding the car. "Come on," he said, helping her out and leading her toward a house that was in the framing stage. "If the night watchman happens along, we'll tell him we're buying this house and we're inspecting the site."

"It smells nice here," Roxie said, breathing in the scent of the freshly cut lumber.

"I love it. I hope I never see the day when we stop using real wood in homes. Here, watch your step. Some jerk left a board there with the nails pointing straight up." Hank bent down and flipped the board over. "That sort of carelessness catches up with you. I see stuff like that and I wonder about the workmanship in the house."

"I'll bet you're a stickler for safety."

"I am, and it appears this company isn't. They have a nice floor plan, though," he added as they walked through the opening that eventually would be the front door. "Spacious."

"Sometimes I like houses better when they're like this than when the walls are finished," Roxie said, looking through the breaks in the studs to the moonlit desert beyond.

"I know what you mean." He glanced into the rafters above them. "Although the flaws stand out more. The grade of lumber's not what I'd use, and I'm not crazy about the joints, either."

"I'd better have you around when I build my dream house," Roxie said without thinking.

"What an interesting thought."

"Hank, I didn't mean—"

He drew her slowly into his arms. "Hey, don't get all flustered about it. Who knows what the future holds for us? You're a mite skittish, Roxie Lowell."

"I suppose I am." She slid her fingers under the lapels of his suede jacket. She'd always liked soft leather jackets on men. The scent of the leather made her think of pioneers and mountain men, rugged individualists. Here, in this partially finished house with sawdust under her feet, the image seemed more real than ever before with this particular man, this builder.

She tilted her head and gazed into his face. In the darkness she couldn't see his expression. Was he as solid as he seemed, or was he a rogue under the clean-cut exterior he allowed her to see? She'd been a terrible judge of character three years ago. What made her think she was any better at it now?

He bent his head toward hers. His lips, slightly parted, slowly merged with hers. He tried to coax her mouth open but she held back, afraid. His pressure grew lighter and he massaged the back of her neck.

Softly he teased her lips with nibbles and tiny flicks from his tongue until the tension drained away and her hands crept up to his shoulders. Finally, with a whispered sigh she relaxed against him and her mouth became a moist cradle waiting to be filled with his kiss.

His arms tightened and his lips settled against hers with a sureness that made her quiver. Once more he'd patiently worked past the barriers she'd erected until he'd found the response he wanted. With a moan she opened her mouth wider to allow his tongue bold exploration of surrendered territory.

The heat from their kiss spread throughout her system as

he blended his body with hers. She didn't need to see his face to understand his emotions now. His kiss and the jut of his pelvis told her exactly what he wanted from her, and Lord help her, she felt an answering ache deep inside.

By the time he lifted his head, he was breathing hard. "I'd better...get you home."

She nodded.

"I don't want to," he murmured, hovering near her again. "I want—damn," he whispered and claimed her hungrily once more.

This time she met him halfway, her lips damp and seeking, her arms wound tight around his neck. She was heedless of self-preservation. Something dark and primitive, something she couldn't have put into words, drove her to this union of mouths and tongues, of secret moisture and shared breath.

The exhilaration of kissing him wiped away her fear of risk and replaced it with a need she dimly recognized. Was it possible that the passion she'd found so difficult to renounce six months ago had been only a weak forerunner of real desire? Dazed and disbelieving, she looked into his face as he lifted his head and shook it once, as if to clear his vision.

"We've got to go," he said, his voice tight and strained. "You're—this was more than I—come on." He grabbed her hand and pulled her gently along toward the car. "I guess Charlie knew what the hell he was talking about," he muttered.

"I guess...he did," she managed to reply.

He tucked her into the seat of the car and fastened her seat belt. She noticed that his hands were shaking, but after all, she was shaking everywhere. *It was just a kiss,* she told herself. *All of Charlie's predictions have worked you into a fever pitch of anticipation. Hank is an ordinary man. This will seem different in the light of day.* But she didn't really believe any of that.

Hank got into the car and sat gripping the wheel and staring out through the windshield. "I didn't really expect that," he said. "You're pretty, and I'm attracted to you, and I wanted to kiss you. I expected to like it, but I didn't think I'd—"

"I know. Me, neither."

"Especially at first, when you were so reluctant to let go."

"I've...just been through a bad experience. That was the main reason I moved out here, to...to recover. I was attracted to you, too, and I was afraid of becoming vulnerable again."

He turned to her, and the moonlight made his eyes glitter. "A married man, right?"

She nodded.

"I thought so, from your reaction about that picture that I dropped. Do you still love him?"

"No."

"Because I'd hate to think you were kissing him instead of me back there."

"I wasn't," she said, gazing at him, thinking of his past. "Who were you kissing, Hank?"

He touched her cheek. "You. Only you. And if we don't start the car I'll do it some more. I think we've found out something. I don't know how much it all has to do with St. Valentine's Day and Charlie Hartman's predictions, but let's not turn our backs on this, Roxie."

"I couldn't even if I wanted to."

"When can I see you again?"

"Perhaps you should answer that. You're the one with two children to consider."

He gave her a rueful glance. "Can't say I was thinking of

them at the moment. And yeah, I've promised them I'd help them with their tree house tomorrow. Would you like to come over and—"

"Not yet," she interrupted gently, laying her hand on his arm. "Another day, maybe, but I have strong feelings about barging in on your time with your children."

He shook his head. "I don't think you'd be barging. They both seem to like you."

"Yes, but—okay, to tell you the truth, I don't want to get too close to those kids until...until I know more about us. I'm trying to protect both them and me, I guess."

"Okay," he said softly. "Monday I have a meeting I can't get out of. Are you free Tuesday night?"

Her pulse raced. "Yes."

"I'll pick you up at seven. Wear something casual."

"All right." Her mouth was dry. A whole evening alone with Hank. His kisses still burned on her lips, and in only seconds she'd been engulfed with desire. What would happen when they had hours?

6

ROXIE SPENT SUNDAY morning on her hands and knees cleaning crusted soap suds off the kitchen floor.

"I wish you'd let me help," Charlie said, twisting his hands as he followed her slow progress around the kitchen. "I feel terribly responsible for the mess."

Roxie sat back on her heels and looked at him. "Well, you are," she said with a smile, "but I understand what happened. It's okay. The floor needed washing anyway."

"I was certain I'd seen you put soap powder in those little cups. Ryan wanted to use the bottle of liquid soap, but I couldn't imagine that was right. When I found the powdered soap next to the clothes washing machine, naturally I assumed..."

"I know. You said all that last night."

"Yes, but I wondered if you'd heard me. You seemed somewhat—" Charlie paused and his eyes twinkled "—distracted."

"Oh, was I?" she replied with great nonchalance as she rinsed out her sponge.

"If I may say so, my dear, you were glowing." Charlie picked out his favorite kitchen chair and sat down. "Ryan and Hilary thought that when you saw the soap all over the kitchen floor you'd—what was their expression?—come unglued, I believe they said. They were amazed at how calmly you took it."

Roxie ducked her head and scrubbed at the dried soap

that had collected in one corner. "As I said, the floor needed cleaning."

"Of course, I would do it all the same again, even including the regrettable incident with the dishwasher. Yes, indeed, all in all I'm quite pleased with my work," he said, almost to himself.

"Your work?" Roxie tossed the sponge into the bucket and gave him a teasing grin. "Are you about to take credit for all that's happened?"

"Perhaps." Charlie shook out his handkerchief and polished his gold pin.

"Well, I guess you were kind of responsible for getting Hank over here, although he might have tried different houses looking for a telephone last Tuesday, and I might have been the only one home, and we might have met anyway."

Charlie cleared his throat in a way that signaled to Roxie that he disagreed with her but was too polite to contradict her outright. "Perhaps," he said, "but I'm always uneasy about leaving those things to chance. Especially with someone like that weasel-faced Doug Kelly hanging around."

"Charlie, really! And after the way you've enjoyed that box of candy that Doug gave me for Valentine's Day!"

"I've eaten the candy to spare you the guilt of eating it yourself, my dear. I thought it might bother you to consume a gift given by a man you never intend to see again, socially, that is."

Roxie put her hands on her hips and gave him a challenging stare. "And how do you know that?"

"Are you?"

"Probably not, but—"

"And Hank?"

She resumed her vigorous scrubbing. "Tuesday night," she mumbled.

"There you have it," Charlie said. "Now, if we could solve poor Como's problem, I'd feel so very much better about everything."

"Charlie, I've warned you about tampering with Como's love life. She's fine. The vet said llama loneliness isn't terminal, and the Osborns will be home by August. They are the ones who should decide what to do."

Charlie stood and walked over to her. "Come and look out the window and tell me she's fine," he said, holding out his hand to help her up.

"What do you mean?"

"Come, come," he said, waving his hand impatiently. "I can see her from here and she's doing it now."

"Doing what?" Her curiosity aroused, Roxie took his hand and got to her feet.

"Pining."

"Oh, for Lord's sake." Roxie peered out the window. "She's looking over the corral fence. That's all she's doing, Charlie, just looking over the fence."

"She stands like that for hours. Did she ever stand there for hours before?"

"I don't know. I never noticed before but maybe I wasn't watching her every move. She might want a change of scenery or something. I'll take her for another walk."

"She wants a sweetheart," Charlie insisted. "You said the Osborns took her somewhere once, the time she wasn't old enough to breed. Was that the direction they went, do you suppose, the direction in which she's staring?"

"Charlie, I haven't the foggiest idea. We are not getting involved in this."

He glanced at her and clucked his tongue. "Roxie Lowell, you are not being a credit to your name with this attitude."

"Hey, I promised to feed and brush and talk kindly to

this llama. I agreed to clean her stall and put down fresh straw. I never said I'd play Cupid.''

"Wouldn't it be lovely to do that, though?"

"No."

Charlie patted her arm. "I know what the trouble is. You don't identify with Como yet. Perhaps in a little while you'll feel differently about her problem."

"And what is that supposed to mean?"

Charlie just looked at her and smiled.

ON TUESDAY NIGHT as she was getting ready for her date with Hank, Roxie had a fresh onset of jitters. She wished that she and Charlie were huddled over the chess table for their regular evening game. Instead, Charlie was in the guest house reading one of the Osborns' books. They had a huge collection ranging from contemporary to classics in fiction, as well as nonfiction books on a number of subjects. Charlie had chosen a study of marriage customs in the Orient and had left muttering something about "catching up on my research."

Roxie had become used to such remarks from Charlie. She had a half-baked theory that he might turn out to be a sociologist in disguise. Perhaps he was writing a scholarly paper on the transients of this country and had decided to live as one for a while. If that were so, she'd be happy for him, but if he was indeed homeless she was determined to provide him with a place to stay for as long as he liked.

In the meantime she had a more immediate concern as she contemplated spending the next few hours with Hank. She'd guessed at what to wear, knowing that the word "casual" covered a multitude of possibilities, especially in Tucson. When she'd first arrived in town she'd attended a party labeled "casual dress" and had seen everything from bathing suits to bow ties. In order to imagine Hank's version of casual she'd relied on his advice and followed her intuition. The result was an emerald, long-sleeved blouse, a gathered skirt with a pattern that reminded her of stained glass windows, and low-heeled shoes.

At exactly seven Hank rang the bell. "Perfect," he pronounced when she opened the door.

"Perfect for what?" she asked, glancing at his cowboy boots, jeans and Western-styled shirt as he walked in. She noticed that he'd worn the suede jacket again and she wondered if he had any idea how sexy he looked in it.

"You'll see in about twenty minutes," he said, gazing down at her. "But take my word for it. Your outfit is just right."

She had trouble focusing on what he was saying while he stood so close to her. Vaguely she remembered his remark when they'd first met about taking her out to try country swing. "Dancing," she said. "Now I remember."

"Right. Country swing. By the way, did you get the soap off the kitchen floor?"

"Finally." She smiled at him. Smiling at Hank was such an easy thing to do. "I knew the chance we were taking leaving Charlie in charge of a major appliance."

He brushed her cheek with his knuckle and gazed down at her with tenderness in his gray eyes. "You should have let me help you with the mess. I would have gladly cleaned up fifty kitchen floors in exchange for those moments with you."

"Absolutely not," she said, trying to keep her voice steady as he stroked her cheek. "Charlie's my responsibility, not yours. I didn't mind, really."

"Speaking of Charlie, where is he?"

"In the guest house curled up with a book."

"And I've been wasting all this time talking about soap."

Hank drew her close and claimed her lips as if he had no doubt of her response.

And he shouldn't doubt it, she thought. His body attracted hers like metal to a magnet. Parting her lips in welcome, she forgot about her carefully applied lip gloss and the five minutes she'd spent combing and fooling with her hair. She forgot about Hank's plan for dinner and dancing as the world shrank to the space within the circle of his arms. She and Hank could have had their entire date in this hallway, for all she cared. Nothing mattered but the pressure of his lips, the thrust of his tongue and the solid urgency of his touch.

"This is crazy," he murmured, releasing her just enough to gaze into her eyes. "All I have to do is kiss you and I forget everything else."

She stayed very still, not wanting to break contact with any part of him. "I know what you mean."

"We really do have dinner reservations, and I want to take you dancing. I like dancing with someone I...someone like you."

She wondered what he'd almost said. It had sounded dangerously close to a declaration of...what? That he wanted her was obvious, but something more glowed in his eyes when he looked at her. She'd noticed that look across the dinner table Saturday night, and across the room during the movie later on. And now. She'd describe it as affectionate, and delighted, and cherishing. Someone who didn't know that they'd just met a week ago might call it a look of love.

But that was ridiculous, she thought. He couldn't love her and she couldn't love him, not so soon. "I'll get my coat," she said, disentangling herself gently. "Are you sure this outfit is okay? I don't look very Western, but I don't have much that fits that description. I haven't bought clothes since I came to Tucson."

"You look fine, wonderful. At this place almost nobody is from Arizona, and the only Western clothes they own are usually what they bought hours ago in the hotel gift shop."

Roxie opened the closet and took out her coat. "Then I guess I'm ready. Unless you'd like a drink or something before we go?"

"No, not really." He helped her on with her coat and combed her hair aside to kiss the sensitive spot behind her ear. "What I want to do is drag you away to a cave."

"By the hair?" she said, disguising her shiver of desire with a laugh.

"No, I never did approve of that method. I'd sling you over my shoulder instead."

The rapid beat of her heart told her that she wouldn't mind if he did exactly that. Forces beyond her control were pushing her toward a point of no return, a point that spelled possible disaster and heartbreak. Yet all he had to do was kiss her and she ignored all signs of danger.

"Back to the subject of hair," Hank said as they left the house. "I'd better ask you about Hilary before I forget. Any chance you could arrange for her to watch someone get a dye job?"

She glanced at him. "You're going to risk it?"

"Yep. Something has to give. She wears that scarf all the time, and after two days at school it looks as if it's been used to clean the playground equipment."

"I'll check with my beautician. Maybe Saturday?"

"That would be great. And I'll pay for whatever she has done, but I'm sure hoping for a return to her regular color."

"Hank, I can't guarantee anything. I wouldn't want you to hold me responsible if—"

"Don't worry. I won't hold you responsible." He helped

her into the car and gazed at her for a moment. "I'll just settle for holding you," he said softly and closed the car door
before she could respond.

They drove north, with the spangled city on their left and
the protective bulk of the shadowy Catalina Mountains on
their right. Roxie had taken this road at night before, but
she wished that she hadn't. Being with Hank was so special
that it seemed as if everything they did together should be
for the first time for each of them. Yet of course many
things, many important things, couldn't be.

She glanced at his profile. He had been married for several years to a woman he loved. She couldn't change that,
or the fact that she'd given her heart to someone else for
three fruitless years. Still Roxie wished that she could wipe
the slate clean.

"Everything okay?" Hank said, taking her hand. "You're
pretty quiet over there."

"I'm fine," she said, giving his hand a squeeze. "What do
you know about llamas?"

He chuckled. "That they're related to camels and that
Kim Novak breeds them. That's about it."

"Kim Novak? Really?"

"Yeah. I read it somewhere. Oh, and I think Michael
Jackson has one living with him, or had at one time. In fact,
I wondered when I first met Charlie if you allowed Como
in the house."

"With those Oriental vases in the living room? Not
likely. She's a sweet animal, but anything that big could
make souvenir mincemeat out of the stuff the Osborns have
collected over the years." She glanced out the window at
the desert landscape. The moonlight made the tall saguaros
and the shorter, segmented cholla cactus seem teddy-bear
cuddly, but Roxie wasn't fooled. She'd picked thorns out of

herself several times since she'd been in Tucson. "Charlie insists that Como is pining away for a lover," Roxie said.

Hank laughed. "That old fellow has romance on the brain, doesn't he?"

"You could certainly say that. The vet told me not to worry about Como, even if she's ready to breed, but Charlie keeps talking about it and making me feel guilty, as if I'm keeping Como from the path of true love. I just wondered what you thought about it."

He glanced at her and smiled. "You're asking the wrong guy at the wrong time if you want me to support you against Charlie. I'm pro romance myself these days."

Roxie thought of what Charlie had said, that she needed a little more time before she'd be able to identify with Como's problem. This was what he meant, of course, being swept along by her feelings for Hank and deciding that every girl, or llama, should have the same good fortune.

"Well, even if the Osborns gave the okay, which they probably wouldn't, I don't want to get involved with Como's love life," she said.

His soft question caressed her. "How about mine?"

"According to Charlie," she replied, flushing, "that's preordained."

"I'm not asking Charlie. I'm asking you."

Her body answered for her as yearning for him spread through her, tumbling her defenses as if they were a row of dominos. "I think Charlie knew what he was talking about," she murmured.

Hank sighed as they turned into the entrance for the El Conquistador Resort. "So do I, lady. So do I."

As they followed the winding drive to a parking area, Roxie discovered that their destination was The Last Territory Steakhouse. The wooden, intentionally rustic building nestled into the hillside a good city block below the elaborate architecture of the main complex.

"I think they put their Western restaurant here so we can smell the stables as we walk in," Hank said as he helped her out of the car. "They want you to get the flavor of the Old West, but of course modern luxury is within shooting distance."

"That fits my idea of roughing it," Roxie said, laughing.

Country and western music and the scent of steak and baked beans seeped into the night as they approached the restaurant. Hank wondered how he'd be able to eat an entire steak dinner when all he wanted to do was take Roxie into his arms. But he'd asked her out, and he'd been raised to believe that a gentleman offers to feed a lady if he has an interest in her.

"Hungry?" he asked as they entered the restaurant.

"Sure."

"That's fine," he said, hoping that his next suggestion wouldn't make him sound cheap. "But the steaks here are huge, and I'd offer to split one with you if you like."

"Oh, yes, please," she said, looking grateful.

He began to hope that she was as reluctant to force down a big meal as he was. That would be a good sign.

The hostess led them past a barrel filled with unshelled peanuts and over to their table. After Hank helped Roxie with her coat and into her chair, he took his seat across from her. The red-and-white-checked tablecloth was anchored in the middle by a knobby red glass container with a candle inside. Hank rested his forearms on the table. Watching the light from the candle flicker in her blue-green eyes, he wondered if she had the slightest idea how beautiful she was.

"You look like Christmas," he said, gesturing toward her emerald blouse and the red-checked tablecloth. He wanted to tell her that she looked like a flame-haired goddess, and that Charlie's descriptions of her paled next to the real thing, but he didn't know how to use such extravagant language.

She smiled and glanced down at the red and green. "So I do. Oh, well, I like Christmas."

"So do I." Hank gazed longingly at the buttons that furrowed between her breasts and disappeared inside the waistband of her skirt. No, he didn't really think of her as a goddess, because goddesses were too ethereal and Roxie was very much flesh and blood to him. The imprint of her body pressed to his was still fresh, like the tracks of a wild thing embedded in a moist riverbank.

Roxie took his breath away, and he hadn't expected that to happen ever again. His need for her was an unreasoning blaze that required only the simple fuel of her lips against his to burst into uncontrolled passion. He shifted his weight and felt the edge of the room key dig into his thigh. He might not use it, might completely waste the considerable sum charged for a night at this resort. Roxie would dictate the terms of the evening, and if he sensed fear or hesitation in her, he wouldn't mention the key.

The waitress appeared and they both decided beer was the appropriate drink for a night among the cowboys. They also ordered one steak dinner and two plates as they'd agreed. The waitress brought two foam-topped glasses of draft and a basket of peanuts from the barrel by the door.

"To broken telephones," Hank said, raising his glass to hers. "Without that we might never have met."

"To broken telephones," Roxie repeated, tapping her glass against Hank's and raising it to her lips.

Hank took a large swallow and put down the glass. "To think I might have worked for months only a block away from you and never known you."

"Doesn't that make you wonder who else you're missing every day of the week?" she asked, licking the foam from the rim of her glass.

"Not now. Not tonight. Are you always this logical?"

"Usually," she replied, giving him a level look.

He liked her intelligence and ability to see all sides of a question, but at the moment he wished she'd put her mind aside and respond to him with pure emotion. "Let's dance," Hank said, holding out his hand to her. The band was playing a ballad about love gone wrong, but Hank refused to be superstitious. Most country and western songs were about love gone wrong, anyway, he figured. The song didn't matter as much as the chance to hold Roxie again.

As they reached the dance floor he drew her close. With the first brush of their bodies she began to relax, and he almost stumbled when she finally snuggled against him as if they'd been dancing this way for years. He held her tight and put his lips next to her ear as they moved slowly around the floor. "I hope you know what you're doing," he murmured, "tucking in against me like this."

She tilted her head back and gazed at him dreamily. Logic wasn't ruling her now. "I'm dancing," she said, her lips curved invitingly. "What are you doing?"

"Oh, nothing," he replied. "Just going crazy. But I expect you know that."

Her pelvis moved against his a fraction of an inch, but it was enough to give him an answer. Joy clamored through him. She was flirting, teasing him into wanting her even more than he already did. And unless he'd misjudged her completely, she wasn't the kind of woman to taunt a man and then pull away indignantly when he asked for more.

He cradled her head against his chest and laid his cheek on the pillow of her bright hair while they slowly circled the floor with the other dancers. He rubbed the small of her back and heard her sigh of pleasure. How he wished that everyone else in the room would disappear.

The dance was exquisite torture as the ache to love her built in him with no immediate promise of release. Yet holding her like this was better than sitting with a table between them. Feeling the fullness of her breasts, the sweet pressure of her hips was worth whatever he had to go through.

The music ended, and he reluctantly eased away from her. They stood on the dance floor applauding politely with the other couples. Hank prayed for another slow tune but knew the chances were against it. Sure enough, the beat picked up and several dancers began the shuffling step used in country swing.

Roxie watched several couples glide and twirl through the fluent movements of the dance before shaking her head. "I can't do that," she said, sounding matter-of-fact once again. "I think we'd better sit this one out."

"No, I'll teach you," Hank said, anxious not to lose the chance to touch her. "It's been a few years since I tried this, but here, take my hands. The step is like this," he said, demonstrating the shuffle going backward and pulling her toward him. "There, that's it. Good. Now you go backward and I'll come forward."

"I feel silly. Everyone else out here dances like a professional."

"You don't look silly," he said. "Now move together and apart to one side, together and apart to the other. Now together and twirl," he coached, catching her around the waist and bringing her close. "You have no idea how the light plays in your hair when you move," he whispered. "God, but you're fantastic."

She smiled at him and the soft expression had returned. "I'll bet you say that to all your students."

"Only the ones with llamas." He guided her through the simple steps they'd mastered and gloried in the way her eyes shone and her cheeks flushed. With Roxie every day would be new, every experience special. It no longer mattered to him whether they used the room key tonight, although he wanted to make love to her desperately. He could wait if necessary, knowing that the moment would come eventually. Sometime in the midst of teaching her this dance he had realized that their fate was inescapable. Charlie Hartman, or whoever he was, had been right on target.

7

By the time the second dance ended, their salads had arrived. Roxie discovered that she had an appetite after all, for all sorts of things—for the creamy ranch dressing she'd ordered for her salad, the tang of the beer and the salted peanuts.

Most of all she had an appetite for the gray-eyed man sitting across from her. The movement and rhythm of the dance had awakened sensual urges in her that she'd almost forgotten existed. Hank's gaze no longer made her nervous; it created a stir of excitement and anticipation.

"Here comes our steak and extra plate," Hank said, sipping on his beer. "When I was growing up my brother and I always had a deal that one person cut whatever food we were sharing and the other one chose."

"We don't need to do that." Roxie moved the candle aside and glanced up at the waitress. "In the middle of the table will be fine, and we won't need the extra plate, thanks."

"This should be interesting," Hank said, leaning toward her.

"Cozy."

"Yeah, I like that." He cut into the steak and smiled at her when their hands brushed. "Friendly, too."

"Umm-hmm." She savored the juicy meat.

"You don't have to answer this," he began as he cut himself another piece of steak, "but I keep thinking about this 'bad experience' you had. I'd like—that is, it would help me if I knew—"

"It's okay, Hank," she said softly. "I'll tell you about him."

He put down his knife and fork and gazed across the table at her. "He really hurt you, didn't he?"

"He sure did," she admitted, returning his gaze. "Mostly he killed my dreams. When I think of how I used to blab on and on to him about how many children I wanted, and what kind of house we'd have, I get furious. By chance I found out that he already had those things, not to mention a wife."

Hank muttered an oath.

"He said, of course, that she didn't understand him, but in reality *I* was the one who didn't understand him."

"Where is this sorry excuse for a man now?"

"In New Jersey still, I suppose, probably looking for another gullible woman."

"He's lucky he's far enough away that it would be inconvenient for me to punch him out. I may schedule a trip back there, anyway."

"Thanks," Roxie said with a wan smile, "but he's not worth the plane fare."

"That may be the only thing that saves him from having his profile rearranged."

"You'd do that, really?"

"He hurt you," Hank replied simply, covering her hand with his, "knowingly hurt you. I have a burning desire to hurt him back."

"I don't know that I've ever had a champion before."

"You do now."

Roxie gazed into the intense gray of his eyes and knew that she was falling in love. Her hunger for the food in front of them was being replaced with the need to touch and be touched. "Let's dance," she murmured.

On the wooden floor she moved into the now familiar haven of his arms with a sigh of contentment. It seemed incredible that a week ago she hadn't known this man. As they swayed together, the warmth of him soaked into her skin and penetrated deep to the place where desire had smoldered all evening. She lifted her head and gazed at him silently.

"It's all been so easy," he said.

"I know."

"But falling in love doesn't have to be difficult."

Her throat constricted and she couldn't answer him. So he felt it, too. The song came to an end and they stood on the dance floor, staring at each other.

"I think I've had enough of this place," Hank said at last. "How about you?"

"It's a little crowded for my taste."

"Then let's go." He motioned to the waitress and quickly took care of the bill while Roxie picked up their coats and her purse. Soon they were standing outside in the cool air and admiring the star-speckled sky. From a shadowed riverbed a pack of coyotes yipped, and down in the corral the horses stomped restlessly in reaction to the coyotes' cries.

"If you block out the view of the resort up on the hill you can almost imagine this is the Old West," Roxie said. "Wild and yet peaceful, too. I have a feeling I'll never live in New Jersey again."

"That's nice to hear." Hank put his arm around her shoulders. "Feel like taking a drive?"

She looked at him and wondered how to say that she longed to cuddle in his arms in a secluded spot away from the rest of the world. She wanted more than that, but she didn't know how, or where to continue this miraculous process of falling in love. "We could take a drive," she said hesitantly. "Whatever you like."

He turned to face her and rested his hands on her shoulders as he studied her quietly. "Listen, I don't know how you'll react to this, but I...reserved us a room. Here. We don't have to go there. It was only a thought, and if you object I'll understand."

Her heartbeat quickened. "You reserved a room?"

"Okay, it was presumptuous of me. I've known you less than a week." He frowned. "Forget it."

Her mind swirled with thoughts of touching him and learning the secrets of his body, of being touched, being filled until the ache in her disappeared. "No," she whispered, running her fingertips along his jaw. "I don't want to forget it."

"You don't?"

"No."

With a shuddering sigh he slipped his hands inside her unbuttoned coat and drew her against him. "Then I wasn't wrong," he said, gazing into her eyes. "You're on this merry-go-round with me."

"I guess I am," she murmured, feeling dizzy at the prospect of loving him.

"When we were dancing, when we were sharing that crazy meal, I wanted to kiss you, touch you like this." Slowly he stroked her breast until it peaked against the material of her blouse. "I want you, every bit of you, Roxie."

She began to tremble in his arms as the sweetness of his caress made her legs rubbery with desire. "Oh, Hank, please don't think of me as less than a lady for wanting you, too, so soon."

His kiss was sweet and lingering, a promise of what was in store when they were alone. "You're my kind of lady,

Roxie Lowell," he said, moving away and leading her to the car.

"There is...one thing," she said as he helped her inside.

He paused and gazed down at her, waiting.

"I didn't seriously consider that we'd—I'm not prepared for this. I don't take birth control pills anymore," she finished in an embarrassed rush.

He smiled. "No problem."

She sighed with relief. He would take care of that, too. She marveled at his courage in making these plans that were so right, yet might have been so wrong, and she thought about his faith in intuition. It had served him well with her so far.

He found a parking space and guided Roxie to the room with such ease that it startled her. "You've been here before," she said, hoping that he hadn't brought someone else to this place.

"Sunday," he answered, relieving her fears. "I took an hour to come over and make sure I knew where everything was." He unlocked the door. "And I hoped," he added, "that I'd be able to use the information."

"It's...very nice," Roxie said, certain that tomorrow she wouldn't remember anything about the room except the enormous bed that seemed to draw all her attention. She walked past it on legs that would barely support her and glanced out the sliding glass doors that led to a small balcony. Beyond was the landscaped interior courtyard of the resort and an opulent pool that glowed turquoise in the darkness.

Hank crossed the room and closed the drapes across the sliding glass doors. He shrugged out of his coat and tossed it on a chair before walking over to her and peeling her coat slowly back from her shoulders. He looked into her eyes. "Second thoughts?"

Roxie wondered why all rented rooms had to smell the same, a vague mix of cigarette smoke, cleaning solution and furniture polish. It wasn't a bad smell, just too familiar. She hadn't counted on the scent of a room to trigger memories she'd rather keep buried forever.

She glanced away. Hank didn't deserve to be lied to. "The, um, married man I was seeing in New Jersey always took me to hotels, I'm afraid. He told me some story about living with a sister who disapproved of sex before marriage."

Hank gently tilted her chin up with one finger. "This man has a name, Roxie. What is it?"

"Mel. His name is Mel." She hadn't spoken his name aloud in six months, and she was surprised at how easily she could say it now. The emotional moments she'd shared with Hank had certainly helped wipe out the pain. If they'd been any place else but this hotel room, Roxie wouldn't have thought of Mel at all.

"Listen, if you're not over him, I understand," Hank said, searching her face for the answer. "But please don't make love to me because you miss him."

"No," she said quickly, laying her hands against his chest. "That's not it," she explained, anxious to dispel his doubts. "When I walked in here I was reminded of him, but I certainly don't want him back. Thinking of Mel now gives me a queasy feeling of betrayal, that's all. I wish I hadn't thought of him in the first place."

"That makes two of us," Hank said, massaging her upper arms. "We don't have to stay. I wouldn't want you to be reminded of that jerk the first time we're together."

Together, she thought, and her skin tingled as she began to forget how the room smelled. "Please kiss me," she said, willing away the uncertainty in his expression. She wanted to see passion there, as it had been before. "Please love me,

Hank." The softness in his gaze faded and was slowly replaced with the heat of desire. "Please," she whispered,
fanning the heat into a flame.

When his mouth deliberately sought hers, she closed her
eyes to focus on her other senses. Unerringly they tele-
graphed the magic of his touch, his scent and the jagged
rhythm of his breathing. She breathed in the musk of passion that surrounded them and opened her lips for his
questing tongue.

His urgency as he fumbled with the buttons of her blouse
sent excitement surging through her. He didn't want to
play games or tease; he wanted the barriers gone as quickly
as possible. So did she.

She helped him with her clothes before they both began
on his. Soon they were flinging garments everywhere until
finally they tumbled, laughing and breathless with anticipation, onto the bed.

"Roxie, my God, Roxie," he mumbled, pressing his lips
against her throat and running his hands with firm pressure over every part of her body. "I want to memorize you.
I want to learn you the way a blind man learns Braille. I
want to know everything there is to know about you,
Roxie."

She moaned as he cupped her breast and brought it to his
mouth. The rhythmic suction of his tongue and lips trans-
mitted a pulse beat through her until she throbbed with
longing. With sure hands he caressed her belly, her thighs,
and at last the moist center where her need for him had become an unbearable ache.

Slipping his fingers between the soft folds, he raised his
head and gazed into her eyes as he stroked her. "Your eyes
are bright as a candle flame," he whispered.

Her answer was a hoarse plea. "I want you."

"Soon." He pushed deeper and settled his lips against

hers, absorbing her whimpering cries. She writhed against him, and as her movements grew more frenzied he slowly withdrew and moved over her.

With one thrust he joined them together. The velvet strength of him entering her at last was all she needed to propel her over the edge. Her hips lifted and she gasped for breath as the undulations rippling inside shook her whole body. A roaring filled her ears, almost blocking out his tender murmured words as he continued to move within her to increase her pleasure.

Gradually the waves of feeling subsided and she realized that his thrusting was less controlled now. She entwined her legs with his and held on tight as he buried himself in her again and again. At last, with a cry, he surged forward one last time and shuddered in her arms.

Her eyes misted as she realized that he'd been concerned with her, with her satisfaction, more than with his. He needn't have worried, she thought. Something about him made her crazy with desire, so crazy that she could think of nothing but this wild surging together, this celebration of physical love.

As she smilingly recreated their lovemaking in her mind, she flushed with the memory of how easily he'd brought her to the brink of release and then given her that release with one swift stroke. Something, however, wasn't quite what she'd expected. And then she realized what it was. Where in their passionate exchange had he taken care of birth control, as he'd assured her he would? Certainly she would have noticed such a thing.

Hank stirred and lifted his head to look down at her. He looked rumpled and very pleased with himself. "Fantastic," he said. "You're wonderful."

"So are you," she replied, tracing his lower lip with her fingertip. "Um, I do have one tiny question, though. You promised to take care of the, uh, protection. Did I miss something?"

He chuckled. "I would say that you don't miss much. I didn't explain all that very thoroughly, did I?"

Roxie fought off an uneasy feeling. Someone like Hank wouldn't treat this subject lightly or put her in jeopardy, she told herself. "Explain what?"

"Fortunately I don't have to worry about such things anymore," he said, kissing her gently. "I'm out of the baby business."

She stared at him and tried to assimilate what he was saying. He couldn't have children anymore?

"You look as if you don't believe me, Roxie. You can believe me. We're okay in that department."

Are we? she thought in a moment of panic. Why did she suddenly feel as if someone had turned out the lights on the Christmas tree? "Well, that's fine, then," she said, clearing her throat of the unexpected catch in it. "I just wondered."

"Sybil and I decided after Hilary was born that two kids were enough, and the operation was far simpler for me than for her. Roxie, is something wrong?"

"No, of course not." She managed a smile. What she was thinking was ridiculous and premature. If she and Hank continued to see each other, and if the subject of marriage came up, that was the time to consider the ramifications of what he'd just told her. For now, they could enjoy a carefree love affair without the risk of pregnancy.

But her argument wouldn't wash. From the moment she'd first kissed Hank, she'd dreamed, hesitantly at first and then with more fervor, of a future with him. She'd included his two children in that hazy picture, of course, but her dreaming hadn't ended there. Roxie wanted a baby of her own.

Slowly Hank levered himself away from her. "I realize

that some people think a man is less masculine after an operation like that," he said, not looking at her.

"Oh, Hank, I don't think that!" Stung by the sad way he'd spoken, she grasped his arm. "I consider your decision loving and responsible. I don't think less of you. If anything, I admire you more."

"Something's changed, though, Roxie." His gaze roved over her face. "I can feel it."

She swallowed. He was far too perceptive and she might as well be honest with him and get it over with. He'd think she was a fool, perhaps, or a marriage-hungry spinster, but that couldn't be helped.

"All right," she said, taking a deep breath. "This is embarrassing to admit, because we've only known each other a short time, but I've already thought about the...future. Yours and mine. Ours."

"That's nice." He gave her a level look. "As a matter of fact, so have I."

"And the thing is, Hank, I've always thought I'd have a baby, or two babies. I love children and always expected to have some of my own."

"I see."

"Oh, damn." She turned her head away. "We shouldn't be having this conversation, Hank. It's silly to talk about babies when we've just begun like this."

He touched her hair. "I don't think it's silly at all."

"Yes, it is." She blinked back tears of disappointment and sadness. "Maybe we'll go out a few more times and discover that we're not really compatible. Then won't we feel foolish, having this discussion when it wasn't even necessary?"

"Now you are being silly. Turn back over here."

She wiped at her eyes and obeyed.

"Roxie," he said, cupping her face in his hands, "neither

of us believes that this is a dead-end street. I don't and I can tell from your reactions that you don't. But we may have hit a speed bump just now, and I think we need to negotiate over it."

She smiled and sniffed. "Sure can tell you're in construction. Dead-end streets and speed bumps. My goodness." His answering grin warmed the cold place that had been developing in her heart. "What do you suggest, Mr. Contractor?"

"I suggest that we keep talking about this, and not bury it like distasteful garbage. And I suggest that you begin spending some time with Hilary and Ryan. They're still children, you know."

"I know. They're delightful children, too." *But they're not mine,* she wanted to add, although she didn't.

Hank stroked her bare arm. "I realize that most women grow up wanting children of their own. There's a conditioning in society toward it. But is it possible, Roxie, that you could learn to love these two children instead?" He held up one hand when she started to say something. "Don't answer me yet. All I'm asking is for you to keep your mind open to the possibility."

She fought against his suggestion. Hadn't she warned herself about becoming the person who filled in the missing space in this little family? She didn't want to slip quietly into Sybil's spot without a ripple. But if she said that, she might start an argument that they shouldn't be having right now.

She caressed his cheek. "Hank, this all seems so...so advanced in thinking from a little while ago, when it was a question of you, and me, and wanting each other. I still feel strange talking as if someday we might..."

"Be man and wife?" he finished softly.

She gazed at him as shivers of emotion skittered up and

down her spine. His wife. The idea was wonderful and threatening at the same time.

"Because we might become man and wife, Roxie Lowell," he said, drawing her against his aroused body. "We just might."

His manhood pressed against her thigh and she trembled with renewed desire. Nothing they'd said had changed her passionate response to him. Probably nothing ever would. "I should be going home," she murmured.

"So should I." He took her hand and guided it downward.

Her fingers closed around him and her thumb gently stroked the satin smoothness of the tip where moisture gathered in answer to her caress.

"God," he whispered, and closed his eyes. "How I crave you, Roxie."

Her heart ached as the confession exposed his vulnerability. "And I you," she said, wanting to even the score, knowing that her needs matched his. "Let me show you how much."

She eased her knee over his thigh and guided him to his back. As she leaned over him, he stroked her breasts until the nipples were stiff and pouting, ready for the pull of his lips and tongue. She lowered her breast to his waiting mouth and watched his cheeks hollow as he took the offering and paid long and tender homage to it. Then she lowered herself over his waiting shaft and initiated a tender rhythm, a loving cadence that was her gift to him.

She meant to follow his example and assure his satisfaction ahead of her own, but the sensuous friction seduced her into an abandon she hadn't intended. He grasped her hips and urged her to an even faster tempo until she was lost and catapulted headlong into a shattering climax. Dimly she heard his groan of release that signaled that she hadn't left him behind. Slick with the moisture of their loving, she lay panting on his broad chest.

Gently he stroked her back, and they were both quiet for a long time. When he finally spoke, it was with a sense of wonder in his voice. "I love you, Roxie," he said. "Lord help me, I already love you."

8

ROXIE CLOSED HER EYES. "It's all happened so fast, Hank. I can't—"

"I know." His unhurried touch on her back subdued any feeling of haste. "Faster for me than for you, I think, but I have less to get in my way. Don't rush the words, Roxie. They'll come. Not long ago you thought love meant hurt and betrayal. I can feel you bracing yourself for the let-down."

She sighed and settled against him. "I guess I am."

"He didn't love you, Roxie. He couldn't have if he lied to you from the beginning."

"That's true, so why was I so stupid?"

"Not stupid," he murmured. "Just wonderfully trusting. That's not a fault. Don't be so hard on yourself."

"All my life I'd depended on logic, except in his case," Roxie continued bitterly. "If I'd used reason instead of emotion, that farce wouldn't have lasted very long." She propped her chin on her fist and gazed at him. "That's what bothers me."

"And why you're afraid to let your emotions take over with me."

She smiled. "Although I can't seem to help it."

"That's what I'm banking on."

She studied his relaxed expression and wondered if she'd ever tire of looking into his clear gray eyes or kissing his tantalizing mouth. Some people meditated by watching the motion of the sea or the shadows of the mountains. She'd be content to look at his face.

That much she knew; that much was simple. It was the rest of the picture that she couldn't assimilate. Loving Hank meant dealing with two half-grown children and apparently giving up hope of having her own. This wasn't the way she'd planned her life at all, and yet...

No one would ever arouse the kind of passion in her that Hank had tonight. She was experienced enough in the ways of desire to know that tonight had been extraordinary. She couldn't push him away, not now, no matter what the problems might be later on.

"You know," he said softly, combing his fingers through her tousled hair, "I love watching your mind work behind those sea-green eyes. Don't ever think that I don't appreciate your logical, intelligent approach to life, because I do. But everything can't be handled that way."

She stayed perfectly still and enjoyed the sensation of his fingers moving through her hair. He could convince her of anything while he was touching her so sweetly.

"Don't give up on your intuition because of one bad call," he continued, slowly massaging her scalp.

"Do you have a dog or a cat?" she asked lazily.

He gave her a startled smile. "What?"

"I just wondered if you have a pet. You're so good at this stroking business."

His eyes grew smoky. "Am I?" Then he sighed. "Damn but I wish we had the whole night together. Or the whole week. Several weeks."

"I suppose it is getting late."

"Yep."

"Hank, what about your children? I hope you don't have some poor teenager staying with them tonight, in the middle of the school week."

"No. Dolores, my housekeeper, stays Monday through Thursday at the house, which is one reason this worked out. But I've never taken advantage of her being there to stay out all night. I don't really care for the image of the single dad who comes dragging in while his kids are having breakfast."

Roxie liked him for caring about such things. "Then it's time for us to leave," she said, easing away from the warm comfort of his body. "You also have to work tomorrow."

"So do you."

"Yes, but I could fall asleep at my desk and nobody would be endangered. If you walk around on the site in a daze, you could be run over by a forklift or something."

He laughed and swung his legs to the floor. "You're cute, but you're also right. Safety is a priority with me, and I've sent guys home who were too tired to watch what they were doing."

"You will be careful, won't you?" She paused in her dressing as she realized that something could indeed happen to him.

"You bet I will," he said with a tender gaze in her direction. "I have lots of reasons not to get run over by a forklift."

During the ride home they talked little but touched often in small, knowing ways. Neither of them wanted the inevitable parting at her door but the moment arrived nevertheless.

"I've been thinking about what comes next," Hank said as they stood on Roxie's doorstep in the circle of each other's arms. "Things are a little complicated with Charlie around here and the kids at my place."

"I know. I halfway expected you to suggest that we come back here after dinner, and even though Charlie's out in the guest house, still I—"

"Yeah. Same here. I made that decision on Sunday, and that's why I reserved the room. Unfortunately even that alternative is limited."

"It sure is. Now that I've had time to think about it, I don't want you staying out late on week nights."

He cupped her behind and brought her in tight against his pelvis. "Not even considering the rewards?"

She closed her eyes as the inevitable pressure built within her. She could feel his quick response, too. "No," she forced herself to say. "Not even considering that."

"Oh, my practical Roxie."

"I don't want anything happening to you."

"You're sweet, you know that?"

She smiled and kissed his chin where his beard was just starting to bristle. "So what are we going to do?"

"Something, that's for darn sure." He thought for a moment. "Tell you what. Sybil's parents live here in town and they've been asking to have the kids for a weekend. This one won't work, because of Hilary's dye job, but the next might. Would Charlie watch over Como if you stayed at my house for the weekend?"

An entire weekend. She couldn't imagine such bliss. "I think he would. I'll ask."

"I think he would, too. In the meantime, why not spend the day with me and the kids this Saturday, after Hilary's hair appointment? We wouldn't be alone, but you can't get to know Hilary and Ryan if we're always alone."

Roxie hesitated as the misgivings she'd tried to submerge surfaced again. "I have this fear," she confessed at last, "that you, and maybe even the kids, will try to mold me into a replacement for...for your wife." She could say Mel's name but she wasn't quite up to Sybil's yet. In the long pause that followed she wondered if she'd offended him and ruined the tender mood they'd established. Her heart thumped in her chest as she prepared herself for an outburst of anger.

Instead he reached up and rubbed the nape of her neck. "The kids might do that," he said in an easy tone. "But I won't, and I'll try to educate them not to. I don't blame you for thinking that, Roxie, but you and Sybil are nothing alike to me. Tonight, when we were making love, I never forgot for one minute who you were."

Roxie began to tremble. God forgive her, she didn't want to think of him making love to anyone else, not even if that person was gone forever. But surely he'd felt the same about her, and yet they'd discussed Mel tonight. He'd been able to put that memory aside and she must take her cue from him. They didn't come to each other shiny and new. Perhaps that added to the richness of what they'd shared, instead of detracting from it.

She wound her arms around his neck and pressed her cheek against his. "I'd love to spend the day with you and the children," she said. "I'll make sure it's okay with Charlie and let you know."

He held her tight. "Trust me, Roxie. Please trust me."

She leaned back and gazed into his eyes, those wonderful eyes that could calm her when she was afraid and excite her when she was not. "Only a fool wouldn't trust you, Hank Craddock."

THE NEXT MORNING Roxie wasn't tired at all. She bounced out of bed earlier than usual, at the exact time, she realized when she looked at the clock, that the workmen arrived at the nursing home under construction down the street. Hank was only a block away. The thought drove her crazy because he might as well have been on the other side of the world. She couldn't drop in on the construction site every day without becoming conspicuous.

She threw on some old clothes and decided to feed Como before taking a shower and getting ready for work. Outside the air was cool and the sky overhead blue as a Siamese cat's eyes. Her steps crunched across the Bermuda grass, a parched tan through the winter although it had been lush and green when she'd arrived in September. She would begin watering it the following month and by August, when the Osborns returned, it would be the same green as when they'd left.

Roxie had wanted everything to appear as if it hadn't changed while the Osborns were gone. With the house, the yard and the llama she might achieve her goal, she thought. But she had changed in the space of one night, and nothing looked the same as it had the day before. The familiar patio, the small adobe guest house, the citrus trees, the corral and miniature barn containing Como's stall—everything looked astonishingly beautiful to Roxie.

She wondered if Hank had fruit trees, and if he would ever consider buying a llama. Hilary and Ryan would love that and Roxie already had some valuable experience in taking care of one. Of course Charlie would have to be a part of the picture she was conjuring up. Hank would have no trouble constructing a small guest house for Charlie.

Roxie considered the full life she'd envisioned and thought that maybe Hank had been right—she might not need children of her own with Hilary and Ryan, and even Charlie requiring her loving care. She quieted the voices that reminded her that she'd never teach a toddler to walk, or record a child's first word, or rock her baby to sleep. Life was full of choices, and she couldn't expect to have everything, she reminded herself.

At Roxie's approach Como meandered out of her stall and over to the corral fence, where she stood with ears pricked forward. Roxie walked toward her and rubbed her soft nose.

"Hi, sweetheart," she crooned, looking into the bottomless brown eyes. "I wish you could be as happy as I am today, but your time will come. Be patient." Como's long white eyelashes flicked down and up, coquettishly, it seemed to Roxie. "Any llama in his right mind would fall head over hoofs for you," she said, scratching behind Como's long ears. "You're so beautiful that you deserve the best, and I'm sure the Osborns will find him."

"Shouldn't Como have a say in the matter?" Charlie commented from behind her. "Surely you don't believe in the sort of arranged matches I read about last night."

"For people or llamas?" she replied, turning to him with a smile.

"Any creature." He walked over to the corral and rubbed Como's long neck. "Any creature should be able to choose."

"Charlie, you are the most romantic person I've ever met. What would you have the Osborns do, entertain gentlemen llamas in the parlor until Como sees one she fancies?"

"Como knows the sweetheart she fancies," Charlie insisted. "I'll wager he's somewhere in that direction," he added, pointing. "The same direction she faces when she stares off into space."

"And I think she likes the breeze there, or maybe the view. Or maybe the fence in that section is just right for scratching a place that itches."

Charlie winked. "She wants to scratch an itch, all right."

"Charlie, you're impossible." Roxie's face grew warm as she was reminded of being in Hank's arms only hours ago. She decided to change the subject. "Anyway, one thing

Como really needs is some breakfast and a little exercise. Maybe I'll take her for a walk."

"Any particular destination?" Charlie's blue eyes twinkled.

"Charlie, you can see right through me, can't you?"

"Yes, my dear, and it's a delightful view. I assume you enjoyed yourself last night."

"Yes." Roxie knew that her color was high, but she couldn't help it. "And as long as we're talking about Hank, I have a couple of favors to ask of you."

"Anything at all."

"Hank has asked me to spend the day with him and his children on Saturday, and I wondered if you'd look after Como for me."

"It would be my pleasure. We'll do some reading. Did you know that she likes poetry? Especially poems about love."

Roxie stared at him. "You read to her?"

"All the time." He pulled a battered leather-bound volume from inside his sport coat. "This is my personal copy of Shakespeare's sonnets. They're her favorites, but I've borrowed some volumes from the Osborns' library, too. Edna St. Vincent Millay was a treat for Como and she really enjoyed Elizabeth Barrett Browning, of course." Charlie grew dreamy-eyed. "Robert Browning and his Elizabeth. Now there is a success story for you. Such lovely people, too."

Roxie shook her head. "I hate to burst your bubble, but Como would probably respond as well to a recitation of the want ads in the newspaper. It's the sound of your voice, not the poetry, Charlie. But I'm sure you enjoy the poetry more, so I don't blame you for reading it."

"Ah, but you're wrong, Roxie. I tried out some Rudyard Kipling on her and she didn't take to it at all."

"How could you tell?"

"It was quite obvious," Charlie said, sticking his thumbs into his vest and lapsing into his lecture mode. "She was restless, always twitching her tail and ears and stomping her feet. She didn't care for Kipling at all."

"Flies," Roxie said.

"There are no flies this time of year," he replied smugly.

"Then maybe she was hungry."

"No. She'd been fed."

"Then...then, I don't know," Roxie said, giving up. "But there has to be a logical explanation."

"There is. She prefers Shakespeare to Kipling."

Roxie threw up her hands. "Whatever you say." At least Charlie's eccentricities were harmless, she thought, picking up a small pitchfork and piling alfalfa in Como's feed trough. "Would you like to read to her while she eats her breakfast?"

"I usually do, while you're getting ready for work in the morning. You're up early today, aren't you?"

"A little." She drew patterns in the dust with the tines of the pitchfork.

"There should be plenty of time for a walk down to the corner and back," Charlie suggested slyly.

"I suppose."

"What was the other favor you wanted, Roxie? You only asked me one, for Saturday."

She wondered now if she could ask him, when the question would reveal the exact nature of her relationship with Hank. But if she didn't ask him, she'd have no way of knowing if he'd be willing to take care of Como for an entire weekend. Maybe he would object to the responsibility.

"Don't be shy, Roxie. What is it?"

"Um, it's about the weekend after this." She glanced at

him furtively. "Hank's children will be away, and he wondered if I—"

"Certainly," Charlie interrupted, sparing her further explanation. "Young lovers need more than a stolen moment here and there. I'll take care of everything here if you'd like to spend the weekend with Hank. I understand that it's the modern way."

"I was afraid that you might disapprove."

"Ah, Roxie." His lined face creased in a smile. "You'll learn that I only disapprove of actions that are born of negative emotions. You can't imagine how pleased I am that you and Hank want to be together. Don't worry about a thing."

"Thank you, Charlie. You're a sweetheart."

"Yes," he said, rocking back on his heels and straightening his red bow tie, "as a matter of fact, I am. Now why don't you go put on a little makeup and brush your hair while I read to Como? Then you can take your walk. I'll warn you, though, that Como will act as if she wants to go in the opposite direction."

"And you think that's where her boyfriend is."

"Naturally. Yours and Como's interests lie at opposite points of the compass this morning, but you take the direction you need to take."

"Don't worry. I will." With a grin Roxie hurried off. She wouldn't do this every morning, of course, but today was special. She needed to see Hank, if only for a moment, before getting on with her life.

Later as she walked toward the construction site she understood what Charlie meant about Como's wish to travel west instead of east, where Roxie wanted to go. Several tugs of the lead rope and some coaxing commands finally got Como pointed in the right direction, but Roxie could tell the llama's heart wasn't in the trip.

Perhaps somehow, Roxie thought, Como had some vague notion that the male llama she'd spurned several months ago could be reached by going west. For all Roxie knew, Como was right, but they certainly wouldn't ever find out. She was sympathetic to Como's plight, but not enough to chance breeding the llama when the Osborns weren't in town.

Roxie kept herself between Como and traffic as they walked along the dirt shoulder of the road. Few cars passed her this early in the morning, but she wasn't about to have Como in any danger. The llama had no fear of cars and her vulnerability made Roxie very cautious.

As they approached the corner, she located Hank's truck immediately, and within seconds she spotted him inside the fence about fifty yards away. He was talking with two of his men as they studied the plans spread out on a pile of lumber. Her heart began pounding faster as she watched him, his head bent over the plans, his arms braced at the edges of the sheets to keep them from rolling up. Her gaze lingered on the hunch of his shoulders and the slant of his hips and she grew warm with remembering.

At the moment when she began wondering how she'd ever make contact with him while he was so engrossed in his work, he looked up and saw her. Even from this distance she could see the white flash of his smile. He said something to the two men, who also turned to look at her. Then he rolled up the plans before walking toward the opening in the fence.

She felt pretty foolish going to meet him with Como in tow, but she'd started this little caper and she couldn't leave now. She didn't want to, anyway. She'd gladly brave the curious glances of Hank's crew and even Hank's teasing for a chance to be with him a few minutes this morning.

And suddenly she knew why. It was the same reason

that she'd been awake at first light this morning, the same reason that everything around her seemed rich with color and fragrant with scent, the same reason that had propelled her down to this corner for a glimpse of Hank. As he stepped outside the fence and drew closer Roxie wanted to run into his arms, and she might have, despite all the onlookers, if she hadn't been leading a llama.

"Hi, beautiful," he said when he was near enough to be heard. "When I first glanced up I thought you might be a desert mirage. In this country desperate men can create what they want to see."

She waited until only a few feet separated them. Then she stopped and took a deep breath. "Hank, I'm in love with you."

He paused and stared at her. "Sometimes desperate men create what they want to hear, too. Would you mind repeating that?"

"I'm in love with you, Hank. I just figured it out. A few seconds ago."

He covered the distance between them in two strides and cupped her face in his hands. His face was shadowed by the yellow hard hat as he gazed searchingly into her eyes. "I can't believe it," he murmured. "Dreams don't usually come true this fast."

She smiled at him. "Sometimes they do."

"I'm a hell of a lucky guy," he said, tilting his head to place a lingering kiss on her lips. "Well, that shoots the day. I was having enough trouble concentrating before, but now..." He gazed at her and shook his head. "What a gift to give a guy on such a gorgeous morning. And I thought last night was something."

"I didn't come here to tell you anything in particular," she said, feeling light as a balloon. "But everything looked different to me today, more vibrant, and I knew that I had to see you. Then when you starting walking toward me, I knew why."

They gazed at each other in wonder until a third face with ears pricked forward and enormous brown eyes entered the magic circle. Roxie and Hank looked at Como and back at each other before they began to laugh.

"Some chaperon you have, lady," Hank said, rubbing Como's neck.

"She didn't want to come along. She thinks that her boyfriend lives in the opposite direction, or so Charlie says."

"At this point I wouldn't discount a word that comes out of that old man's mouth."

Roxie laughed. "Neither would I."

"Which reminds me, did you ask him about taking care of this beast?"

"Yes, and he'll be glad to do it." Roxie slackened the lead rope and Como found a small clump of weeds to munch on. "Charlie reads Shakespeare's sonnets to Como, by the way, and he swears she has a taste for classical poetry, especially on the subject of love." Roxie paused, not wanting to seem disloyal to the old man whom she cherished. "Hank, don't take this wrong, but do you think Charlie's um—"

"Unbalanced? Not in any way that will cause trouble. And sometimes people who are a little crazy see things that others miss. Charlie knew in his bones that we'd be right together, and with those credentials he can teach Como to play the bagpipes, for all I care. He's earned the right to follow his instincts, in my book."

"Then I'll stop worrying."

"And start planning," Hank said. "Sybil's folks are available this weekend and not the next, so if the beauty shop thing can be scheduled early this Saturday, I'll take the kids over to their grandparents' house in the afternoon."

"This weekend?" Roxie's heart thudded with excitement.

"And it's a good thing, too, because I'd decided that life was going to be pretty frustrating if we had to wait another week to be together. In fact, I've been plotting how we might steal a few hours on Thursday night."

"You have? But I thought we said—"

"I know what we said, but I want you so much that it's tearing me apart. And especially now..." He stroked her arm. "I have an idea, and it has nothing to do with a hotel room. I also decided that I'll have no more of following in your friend Mel's footsteps."

She touched his cheek. "Believe me, there's no danger of that."

"Still, we're through with hotels."

"Hank, if you're considering a rendezvous outside, I'm scared to death of snakes and bugs and things."

"Not outside."

"You've really aroused my curiosity."

"I'd like to arouse more than that," he said with a wink. "Can I pick you up then on Thursday?"

"I wouldn't miss it for the world. If we're not going to your place or mine, or to a hotel, or out in the boondocks, what could you have in mind?"

"A trick of the trade, literally. And I hate to say it, but I have to get back to work."

"I know. I really didn't mean to keep you so long. I just wanted—"

"Lord, don't apologize for the most wonderful thing that could have happened to me in a month of Sundays." He cradled her head and tipped it back for a fleeting kiss. "Thursday at seven, my beloved Roxie of the flame-red hair and sea-green eyes."

She watched him lope back through the fence. He turned

once and waved, and she waved back. Then she disengaged Como from her clump of weeds and walked home in a daze. She wondered how she'd ever make it through the endless hours until she was with Hank again. She had no clue as to where he was taking her on Thursday, but it didn't much matter. Contrary to what she'd said, she'd lie in the middle of the desert on a blanket, with wild creatures everywhere around her, if Hank's arms held her tight.

9

ON THURSDAY NIGHT Roxie dressed in a gold velour sweat suit. She still suspected that Hank's plans had something to do with the great outdoors. He worked an outside job, she reasoned, and he looked like the sort of man who would own a tent and an inflatable mattress. When he arrived in jeans, running shoes and a gray sweatshirt, she became even more convinced that she was right.

"I think you've guessed where we're going," he said, gathering her close for a kiss before they left.

"I think maybe I have." She reveled in his assured manner. On Tuesday he'd been uncertain how the evening would progress. Tonight he knew, and the difference was in his eyes, in his kiss, in the way he molded his body to hers.

"Let's go," he murmured. "The past two days have been an eternity."

"Do I need anything, like maybe a flashlight?"

"I have candles."

"A coat?"

"This sweat suit should be warm enough at first, and after that, I'll keep you warm." He kissed her once more, hard, and they hurried out the door.

"This will be a new experience for me," Roxie said as they drove away.

"For me, too."

"Really?"

He laughed. "Yes, really. What sort of Romeo do you take me for?"

"Well, I thought maybe...when you were married."

"When I was married there was no need for this kind of stunt. But I must admit it's been fun, planning it. I have a picnic hamper in the back with some wine and some goodies from the deli." He glanced at her when they stopped for a traffic light. "If we want to take time for such boring things as eating, that is."

A thrill of anticipation traveled through her, tightening her nipples and warming the intimate place between her thighs. She gazed at him without speaking.

"I think maybe we'll forget the food," he murmured and sped through the intersection.

Roxie expected them to drive away from civilization and head for one of the campgrounds at the base of the Catalina Mountains, but instead they drove toward an expensive housing development. "Hank," she said uneasily, "we're not having this picnic in your backyard, are we?"

He chuckled. "So, you didn't guess, after all."

"I figured we'd spend the evening in a tent, and I was praying that it had a floor and flaps that zipped tight."

"You said you didn't like bugs or snakes, so I wouldn't have considered a tent. Even floors and zippers don't completely solve the problem of critters in the desert. The only tickle on your skin you'll feel tonight will be me." He turned down a dirt road that ended at a house half-hidden in a grove of mesquite trees.

"Where are we?"

"A good friend of mine is building this house and hopes to sell it for a lot of money. They put down carpeting yesterday and I'll be in deep trouble if we spill wine on it. But Ed trusts me and also owes me a few favors, so he said the house was mine for the evening. He knows I'd replace anything that was damaged, anyway."

"Your friend knows why you wanted the key?" In the darkness Roxie flushed and hoped never to run into this person named Ed.

"He's a good guy, Roxie. I've known him and Joanie for years, and when I told him I'd met a lady with an aversion to hotel rooms, he slapped me on the back and said 'It's about time.' He said that giving me the key made him feel like Cupid."

She turned in the seat and looked at him. "He hasn't been talking to Charlie, has he?"

He smiled. "Not that I know of. Come on, now, Charlie can't be responsible for everything good that happens to us. He's not a magician."

"You're right, but sometimes it seems spooky the way things fall into place for us. Saturday morning, for example—the early hair-coloring appointment that just happened to be available for Hilary to watch. You know that I'm not superstitious, but—"

He squeezed her hand. "I say let's enjoy it. Whether it's fate or coincidence, we're here tonight, and we have most of the weekend together."

"I know. Sometimes I pinch myself to make sure I'm awake."

Hank opened the car door. "I don't," he said softly. "If this is a dream, I don't want to know it." As he helped Roxie out of the car he handed her the house keys. "I'll carry the hamper in if you'll open the door. And watch out for boards and pieces of wire lying around, although Ed's usually pretty careful, and he knew we'd be coming here in the dark."

"What about the neighbors? Won't they wonder what's going on if they see lights and hear voices?"

"There's enough acreage around the house that the neighbors, what few there are, wouldn't even notice."

There were two keys, one for the door lock and one for a dead bolt. Roxie felt her way through the process of opening both locks and turned the brass doorknob. Their steps echoed as they walked through a tiled foyer.

"Which way?" Roxie asked as her eyes adjusted to the dim light.

"Down there, in the sunken living room, where the moonlight is coming through that big window. We won't even need the candles." Hank led the way down three carpeted steps and over to a beehive fireplace. He set the wicker hamper on the raised hearth and turned to her. "What do you think?"

"Everything smells so new." She gazed up into the shadows of the beamed ceilings. "I like this house. I like the feeling of it."

"Ed's a good builder." Hank took a soft blanket from the wicker basket.

"I can understand why you're friends. This house has an atmosphere of caring in it."

"That's right." Hank spread the blanket in the square of moonlight coming through the floor-to-ceiling picture window. Then he took her hand and pulled her down beside him. "The perfect atmosphere for loving you," he said gently, easing Roxie back on the blanket.

"And you," Roxie murmured, and arched against him as his lips found hers.

Hank prayed he wasn't dreaming this moment of holding Roxie and breathing in the fragrance of her skin. If he could design a dream it would be like this, with her mouth sweet and damp, her breast filling his hand when he reached under her sweatshirt and unfastened the front clasp of her bra.

She moaned as he rolled her taut nipple between his thumb and forefinger. All men did dream of this, he thought, of a woman who wanted you so much that she pushed the weight of her breast against the palm of your hand. Beneath the swell of her flesh he felt her heart beating wildly as he stroked the depths of her mouth with his tongue.

"Roxie, Roxie," he murmured, saying her name between kisses that probed the delights of her honeyed mouth. He paused only long enough to pull the sweatshirt over her head. Her bare breasts gleamed in the moonlight splashing in through the window. The rest of her clothing seemed a sacrilege and he took that away, too.

"God," he breathed. "I love you like this."

She smiled, a voluptuous, siren's smile. "You could love me better if you'd take off your clothes."

He did, never removing his gaze from the sight of her, her pale skin silvered by the moon except in the secret, shadowed places that drove him insane. He sank back to the blanket and sent a silent thanks to his friend for putting in the best carpet money could buy. The soft pile gave under his weight like a foam mattress. He could love this woman as forcefully, as deeply as he wanted, as she wanted, and not worry about hurting her.

He touched her lightly at first, as he would a valuable porcelain vase. He began at her throat and stroked downward with the back of his hand. His knuckles rubbed over the heated surface of her skin in a gentle massage that moved past her collarbone and circled over each breast.

He watched her face. Her pupils grew to black pools as he continued his caress down her ribs and across her taut belly. Her lips parted and her breathing became uneven. He stroked the inside of her thighs and felt the restless motion of her hips.

"Hank," she whispered, telling him with her gaze what she wanted.

"There's more," he murmured, and touched his lips to her throat. He drew the journey out, testing himself to see how much he could stand. He raked each nipple gently with his teeth until her chest was heaving. When she buried her fingers in his hair and arched upward he took her fully into his mouth. Her pliant flesh made him dizzy with wanting her, but he held back. He wanted her to remember this night for a long time, perhaps for the rest of her life.

Releasing her breast slowly, he pressed his lips to the valley between her ribs. He traced a path downward with flicks of his tongue moistening her pearly skin until it glistened in the pale light. When he kissed the inside of her thigh, she gasped.

She was velvet rich and drenched with passion. The taste of her nearly pushed him beyond his power to control the throbbing in his groin. She cried out and writhed against the blanket as he loved her, and he had to grasp her hips to keep her still, but he kept on until he became mindless with the need to be inside her.

Her cries became husky, urgent. "Hank...now, please, Hank..."

No longer able to resist her pleas, he levered himself up on his outstretched arms and pushed deep into her. Nothing on earth could have kept him from it. With each thrust she trembled against him and dimly he realized that the same force of passion was raging to be loose in her, too.

Again and again they came together, each time more explosive than the last. He knew they were there. Once more. He thrust forward and they became the grand finale on the Fourth of July. He wrapped his arms around her and held on as spasm after spasm wracked his body and hers.

He lost count of how many times he told her he loved her

and how many times she vowed her love to him. He never tired of saying or hearing those words. The truth of them was reflected in their damp, heated bodies that had, for a moment, been one.

At last he tightened his arms around her and rolled them both to their sides, facing each other. "I love you," he said again. "I can't think of anything more important to say than that. I love you, love you, love you."

"And I love you." Her voice was husky. "There isn't anything more important to say."

He gazed at her for a long time. "There might be one thing more to add."

"What?" she asked softly.

"Marry me."

She didn't answer him.

"Maybe...maybe you're not ready for that question."

"Hank, I—"

"No. Never mind." He placed a finger across her lips. "You love me. That's enough for now. Don't think about the other yet."

ROXIE DID THINK OF IT, though. She thought of it while they sipped on the wine and ate from the plastic cartons of salad and meat he'd brought. She thought of it after they made love again and during the drive home, and while she sat at her desk on Friday.

She thought of his proposal almost constantly, because she'd almost said yes. If he'd left the silence alone for another second she would have agreed to be his wife, but when he'd spoken she'd known that he was right. She wasn't ready for the question.

Her lack of readiness had nothing to do with Hank. He was everything she wanted in a husband and lover. But for Roxie, the word *marriage* had always been paired with the word *family*. Hank's family came ready-made, with no additions allowed. She'd have to become an instant mother to Ryan and Hilary and give up the notion of her own baby, or more exactly, hers and Hank's baby. That idea was tough to relinquish, because Roxie believed that having a baby together was an important way for two people to express their love.

Charlie hadn't commented on Roxie's self-absorption all day Friday until the two of them sat down for a chess game. Within the first three moves he chuckled and laid his hand on hers. "Maybe we should rent a film tonight instead of playing chess, my dear. Your brain seems taxed beyond its limits."

Roxie frowned. "What's the matter?"

"You seem to be working both sides of the board tonight. You just moved my queen."

"I did?"

"I wouldn't have mentioned it, except that you put the poor lady within capturing distance of your knight. Is there a significant message in that?"

She looked into his kind face, lined with years of experience in living, and decided to ask his advice. "The thing is, Charlie," she began, leaning back into the winged armchair, "that last night Hank asked me to marry him."

"Capital! I'm so pleased." All of Charlie's wrinkles creased at once as he beamed at her. "If you're worried about the brief span of your acquaintance, let me put your mind to rest, dear child. This union will be a solid one, Roxie. You can trust me on that."

"I'm not worried about not knowing him well enough, Charlie. To tell you the truth, I feel as if I've known him forever. It's—another problem." She picked up the knight from her side of the chess board and turned it around in her fingers. "The matter of children."

"You'll get along fine with Hilary and Ryan. You'll all have to grow used to one another, and there will be the normal sorts of catastrophes, but don't forget that they also bear the Craddock name and are therefore abounding in love. They need to lavish that affection on someone besides their father, and you need children to nurture. It will be a very satisfactory arrangement." He whipped out his handkerchief and polished the gold figure-eight pin on his lapel, as if he had just dispensed with all her possible objections to the marriage.

"You don't understand, Charlie. Hilary and Ryan aren't the biggest problem, although I have to consider if I'm ready to be the mother of an eight- and ten-year-old. But I imagine that will work out, as you said. They're nice kids."

"With a father like Hank, how could they be otherwise?"

"I think," Roxie said with a tiny smile, "that their mother deserves some credit, too."

"Well, of course she does. I suspect that she was a fine woman. Is that what's bothering you, Roxie?"

"Some, to be honest. If she was a good wife and mother she may be elevated to sainthood by now. People do that sometimes. Don't forget that Hilary wants to dye her hair to be more like her mother."

Charlie leaned across the chess board and patted Roxie's knee. "If anyone but you were following in her footsteps, I might be concerned. You, however, won't live in the shadow of Hank's late wife. I know you and I know Hank, and there's a flame burning between the two of you that is brighter than anything either of you has experienced before."

Roxie put the knight back on the board and gazed at him intently. "I'll admit that's true of me, but how can you know that about Hank? He loved his wife very much, I think."

"Yes, he did, but he's obsessed with you. It's not the same at all. He told me so this morning."

"You talked with him?"

"Briefly. I strolled down to the site while you were in the shower. We had a friendly chat, and he thanked me for bringing you two together. He said that you were the most exciting woman he's ever known, both mentally and physically." Charlie gave the pin a last swipe with the handkerchief.

"My goodness," Roxie put her hands to her warm cheeks as she remembered how Hank had loved her last night. "I can't imagine him saying all that to you."

"Why not? Hank and I understand each other."

"Then if you're such pals, did he mention that if we marry, our family will stay the same size because he can't have any more children?"

Charlie's benevolent smile faded. "I beg your pardon?"

"I thought not. That's what I've been brooding about all day, Charlie. You see, wonderful as Hilary and Ryan are, they won't ever be my children. I've always looked forward to having a baby of my own, and now that I've fallen in love with Hank the urge is more specific. I want his baby, but that's impossible."

"Impossible? I don't understand."

"Surely you've heard of vasectomies. After Hilary was born, Hank and his wife decided not to have any more children, so Hank had an operation."

Charlie became agitated. "But Roxie, I certainly hope that he still can perform the usual acts of—"

"Yes," Roxie said, flushing. *Could he ever!* "But no children will result. That's the point of the surgery. Lots of men do it these days." She glanced at Charlie. His consternation would have been funny to watch if she weren't so emotionally involved in this problem. "So you see, my valentine lover isn't as perfect for me as you once thought. He has a flaw."

Charlie mopped his forehead with the handkerchief and sighed. "Confounded modern science," he muttered, as if to himself. "How can I be expected to keep up? Things were difficult enough when some fool invented the chastity belt, and now this."

"Charlie?" Roxie peered at him in concern. "What on earth are you talking about?"

He looked up but he wasn't focusing on her. "There must be an answer," he said to the room in general as he stood and wandered over to the bookshelves lining one wall of the room. "I believe the Osborns have a medical encyclopedia. Ah, here it is." He reached inside his jacket for his reading glasses and perched them on his nose. Then he took the book from the shelf and began thumbing rapidly through the pages.

Roxie stared at him. Whatever reaction she'd expected of Charlie, it hadn't been this. She'd thought that he would counsel her to accept the situation, or to consider adoption. Instead he was behaving as if Hank's operation were a personal affront that had to be dealt with immediately. And what was that nonsense about chastity belts?

"Aha!" Charlie closed the book with a snap and marched back to her. "The operation," he announced, removing his glasses with a flourish, "can be reversed."

Her mouth dropped open. Admittedly she hadn't thought of that possibility, but could she even ask it of Hank?

"Doesn't that solve the dilemma, Roxie?"

"I'm not sure. I remember now that such a thing is possible, although the operations aren't a guaranteed success."

"This one will be," Charlie said, tucking his glasses away. "You and Hank will have that baby you want."

"That's just it. I don't know if Hank wants another child. Plus I'd be asking him to go through another operation, which is no fun, I'm sure."

"But this is important to you, isn't it? You've been dreadfully distracted all day. You simply must ask Hank about this, Roxie. I'm certain everything will be fine."

"You're quite an optimist, Charlie," Roxie said, but she felt better now that a possible solution existed. Perhaps she could have everything she wanted.

"You and Hank will straighten everything out this weekend," Charlie said with conviction. "I have confidence that—"

He was interrupted by the telephone and Roxie hurried to answer it. Perhaps Hank had found a moment to call her. She decided while picking up the receiver in the kitchen that she wouldn't bring up the matter of babies over the telephone, though. It was too important a question to be tossed out in the middle of a casual phone call.

Roxie knew as soon as she heard the crackle of a long-distance line that the caller wasn't Hank.

"Roxie? This is Fran," a woman said. "How are things going?"

"Why, uh, fine—just fine!" Roxie hadn't talked to the Osborns since Charlie had moved in, and her head whirled as she realized how much had happened in a short time. "I've invited a dear old friend to use the guest house," she said, choosing not to be specific about Charlie right now.

"That's perfectly all right. We told you to do that if you liked. How's Como?"

"She's...okay. I called the vet because she seemed a little listless, and he said that she's in season. But he said not to worry, that she'll be fine until you come home."

"In season? Really? How exciting! Dave and I really do

want to breed her. Wouldn't that be cute, to have a baby llama running around?"

"Yeah, it sure would," Roxie agreed, picturing a miniature version of Como. She'd like to see that, herself, but then she was slightly fixated on babies these days. "Anyway, you should be able to try breeding her when you get back."

"We certainly will. I can hardly wait. We have her boyfriend all picked out. Any other news?"

"Oh, not really." Roxie couldn't imagine how to explain that she'd fallen in love within the space of two weeks; that subject was best kept under wraps for now. "How is the trip going?"

"To tell the truth, we're becoming a tad travel weary, but we'll probably stick it out to the end. I've told Dave that next time we'll go for a shorter time. Maybe I'm getting old, but I miss my own kitchen and bathroom."

"I can understand that. This is a lovely house."

"Well, we're lucky to have you there caring for it. You're sure Como will be okay?"

"The vet assured me that she would."

"Don't hesitate to call him again if necessary. Dave and I don't mind the expense, and there should be plenty in that emergency fund we left for you."

"Yes, there is, but I shouldn't have to call him again. She's not sick."

Fran laughed. "Just lovesick. Okay. Give her a big hug for us, then, and I'll call you again in a couple of weeks. And thanks again for everything."

"You're welcome. Goodbye." Roxie hung up the phone and returned to the living room where Charlie was sitting at the chess board once more. "That was Fran Osborn. I told her that a dear friend was staying in the guest house and that Como was in season."

"And that you were in love?"

"No, I didn't mention that."

"Ahh." He gazed at her. "You still can't quite believe it, can you?"

"I guess not."

"No matter. This weekend should take care of your doubts. What did she say about Como?"

"She's delighted. They have a boyfriend all picked out for her and they'll breed her when they come home."

"That seems rather arbitrary."

"Charlie, she's a llama."

"A creature who appreciates Shakespeare is not to be treated so cavalierly. Como has delicate feelings."

Roxie sat down on the other side of the chess board. "Delicate feelings or not, she doesn't belong to either one of us, and the Osborns have the right to decide what they'll do about breeding her." She glanced up in time to catch the rebellious expression on Charlie's face. "I mean it, Charlie."

His face relaxed into a smile. "Of course, my dear. Of course."

10

HANK BROUGHT HIS DAUGHTER to Roxie's house by eight the next morning and turned Hilary over with such confidence that Roxie was touched. Then he and Ryan left for batting practice in preparation for Little League tryouts the following week. The four of them could have been an average middle-class family separating for the usual Saturday-morning activities, Roxie thought. She didn't mind at all.

"How long will I have to watch this other lady get her hair bleached?" Hilary asked as she and Roxie drove the short distance to the beauty shop.

"Georgia, my hairdresser, said it could take two and half or three hours. Of course, you don't have to watch all of it, unless you definitely decide to have yours done the same way." Roxie glanced at Hilary belted in beside her. The blue and lavender scarf, its original beauty obscured by five days of playground dust, was knotted under her chin. No matter what color her hair became, it would be an improvement over the bedraggled scarf.

"Then I'll have to watch all of it," Hilary said with a resigned sigh. "Because I'm going to have blond hair today for sure."

"Okay." Roxie wondered if Hilary would go through with the whole procedure, after all. She was a determined little girl, but Georgia had assured Roxie that the process was sufficiently obnoxious to discourage Hilary from having it done. Georgia, Roxie and Hank had prepared for both contingencies. If Hilary decided to stay an additional three hours and have her hair bleached, Roxie would call Charlie and Charlie would alert Hank when he returned with Ryan.

Roxie swung the Volvo into the shopping center, the same one where she and Hank had rented the movie their first night together. "Here we are."

"I've seen this place before," Hilary said with worldly disdain. "This is the same place we get movies."

"That's right. Your dad rented the one we saw last week here." Roxie switched off the ignition. "Ready?"

Hilary nodded vigorously. "Yes." After she got out of the car, she thrust back her shoulders and smiled in anticipation as Roxie led her into the shop.

Roxie wished for a moment that hair dyeing weren't such a difficult, uncomfortable process and that Hilary could have what she wanted. She regretted having to dash the child's joy, but it couldn't be helped. After Georgia had described the procedure in detail over the phone, Roxie had known that such a thing was not appropriate for an eight-year-old.

Georgia greeted them from her station. "Come on back," she said, brushing the hair of a woman in her late thirties or early forties. "Judy says she'll be glad to have Hilary as an audience. I've got a chair all set for her."

"I appreciate this," Roxie said to both women. "Hilary wants so much to have this done, but she has no idea what's involved."

Judy, whose dark hair was shoulder length, made a face. "A lot's involved," she said to Hilary. "I'd wait a few years if I were you, sweetheart."

"I don't want to wait," Hilary replied, clutching Roxie's hand. "I want my hair bleached today, right after yours."

Georgia glanced at Roxie as if to reassure her that Hilary

would change her mind. "Well, just sit on that chair," she said to Hilary, "and watch how it's done. Roxie, you can sit at Tina's station. She's not working today."

"That's okay," Roxie said. "I'll stand for a while." She released Hilary's hand, and the little girl marched over to the armless vinyl chair assigned to her. When she discovered that the seat swiveled, she began to spin from side to side.

"Just remember," Georgia said, pausing in her task of parting Judy's hair to glance at Hilary, "that when you have your hair bleached you won't be able to move like that. You'd better practice sitting very still."

Hilary stopped turning immediately and gazed at Georgia with wide eyes. "Okay."

Roxie leaned against the wall and thought how lucky she was that Georgia had two daughters and knew something about little girls. Roxie hoped that Georgia knew them very well.

"Now, Hilary, this is the first step," Georgia said as she opened a bottle and squeezed a creamy liquid onto a section of Judy's hair.

"Phew, it stinks!" Hilary said, holding her nose.

"Can't be helped," Georgia replied, continuing to work with the liquid.

"It stinks more than the stuff I used," Hilary added in a nasal tone while still holding her nose. "How long does that have to stay on?"

"Oh, quite a while," Georgia said.

Judy held a towel over her nose. "I'll tell you something else," she said, her comments muffled by the towel. "When it gets on your skin it stings."

Roxie glanced at Hilary, who was showing signs of dismay.

"Stings?" Hilary asked. "How much?"

"Sort of like a bee," Judy answered.

Hilary shivered. "I got stinged by a bee once. Boy, it sure smells bad, doesn't it?"

"That's ammonia," Georgia explained. "We need something this strong to take all the color out."

"I didn't know it would stink so bad." Hilary covered her mouth and nose with cupped hands and breathed into them while she watched Georgia work with growing anxiety.

"Does the other stuff smell like this?" Roxie asked casually, as if she hadn't covered this topic thoroughly with Georgia over the telephone. "The stuff that would make Hilary's hair brown again?"

Georgia shook her head. "Not even close. The semipermanent color smells more like Elmer's glue."

"We have Elmer's glue at home," Hilary said, her statement echoing in the chamber of her cupped hands.

Roxie said nothing more and allowed the smell of the ammonia to work on Hilary for several minutes. Roxie could barely stand it herself, and she kept dabbing at her watering eyes and wondering how Georgia managed to work with such strong chemicals all the time.

"How much longer?" Hilary asked after a while, taking her hands away and then clapping them back over her nose and mouth.

"At least another half hour," Georgia said. "I still have to work the solution down to the roots and out to the ends. Didn't Roxie tell you we wouldn't be completely finished for almost three hours?"

Hilary nodded. "But I didn't know it would stink so bad," she said through her hands.

Roxie tossed Hilary the next piece of bait. "How long does the semipermanent hair color take to apply, Georgia?"

"If someone sits very still, I can have that person out the door in thirty minutes."

Hilary glanced in surprise at Roxie. "That's not so long to sit still."

"Of course you'd have to finish Judy's hair before you could do anything, right, Georgia?" Roxie said, knowing the answer to that, too, from the telephone call.

"Oh, I could work someone in, if all they wanted was a semipermanent coloring job," Georgia answered.

"But I guess Hilary doesn't want that," Roxie said.

"Yes, I do!" Hilary said, jumping from the chair. "It stinks too bad in here!"

Under cover of Judy's amused chuckle, Roxie sighed with relief. The plan had worked. Roxie felt mentally exhausted and decided she didn't need to supervise every minute of this process, now that the crisis was past.

As Georgia bustled about settling Hilary in a booster seat at Tina's station, Roxie touched Hilary's arm. "I'm going to read a magazine up front, if you'll be all right back here."

"Sure." Hilary had obviously decided that Georgia could be trusted. "I'll be okay."

"Yeah," Georgia agreed. "Go relax for a while. Hilary and I will do just fine together."

Grateful for the break, Roxie found a chair in the reception area and leafed through the magazines on a corner table. At least three had articles about "stepfamilies." She'd heard the term before but hadn't paid much attention because she'd never expected it to apply to her life. This morning she was hungry for information.

The articles assured her that with time, the children in stepfamilies would adjust with the love and support of their natural parents and their stepparents. Roxie hadn't really doubted that part. Ryan and Hilary had been adjusting ever since their mother's death. Perhaps by now they were better at giving up old dreams and creating new ones than she was.

Their expectations weren't the problem; hers were. She stopped reading and sat with the open magazine on her lap. She thought of the wonder of being in Hank's arms and weighed it against the problems of adapting to a ready-made family with its daily reminders that another, well-loved woman had been there before her.

The children missed their mother, would always miss her, but logic told Roxie that in time Sybil would become less of an influence in their lives. Roxie wouldn't feel like an interloper forever.

Then she thought of Charlie's suggestion—that Hank's operation be reversed so that he and Roxie could have a child of their own. The more Roxie considered the idea, the more she believed in its worth. She longed to be the mother of Hank's child, but the arguments for having a baby went beyond satisfying her desires.

A baby would alter the basic structure of Hank's family and create something entirely different. Roxie wanted that very much, for the same reasons that she'd rearranged the furniture in the bedroom she used in the Osborns' house. By changing the composition of the family, she could make it hers.

With a sigh Roxie closed the last of the three magazines and put them all back on the table. A tall planter box blocked her view of Georgia's station and she couldn't see what was happening to Hilary, but she could hear the little girl's voice as she chattered happily to Georgia.

Hilary would be an easy child to love, Roxie thought. She hoped it wouldn't be very long before Hilary loved her back. Roxie knew she couldn't expect the same fierce emotion that Hilary felt for her mother, though. For that, Roxie would need a child of her own. She leaned toward the corner table and picked up a fourth magazine that featured an article on breastfeeding.

A short time later she heard giggles from Hilary and exclamations of pride and wonder from Georgia. Roxie glanced up as they both paraded into the reception area with Hilary in front, walking as if she were an heir to the throne, and Georgia following a worshipful distance behind.

"I'm ready to go now," Hilary declared and paused dramatically beside the cash register counter.

"My goodness, how beautiful you are," Roxie said. Georgia had not only returned Hilary to her original color but given her a shorter cut that emphasized her large gray eyes. The longer hair, in a style similar to her mother's, had been a mistake for the shape of Hilary's face.

"And I'm not even blond," Hilary responded proudly.

"No, but you're certainly spectacular," Roxie said. She took the money that Hank had given her out of her purse and handed it to Georgia. "You did a wonderful job."

"Thanks. It is nice, if I dare say so myself. She's a lovely young lady."

"Absolutely." Roxie glanced at her watch. "We'd better head back to my house, Hilary. Your dad and Ryan will be there any minute."

"I can hardly wait to show them!" Hilary lost her regal poise and jumped up and down. "They won't believe I look so good. Then I get to show my grandma and grandpa."

"So you do." Roxie hadn't even considered Sybil's parents in this complicated situation, but they would continue to be a part of Hilary and Ryan's lives, of course. If she accepted Hank's proposal she would meet them soon. There might be talk of old times. The references would be polite, not designed to hurt perhaps, but they would still indicate a past in which Roxie had played no role. She hoped that she could handle it.

On the ride home she kept glancing at Hilary, who really

didn't look like the same child. When they reached the Osborns' house Charlie hurried out to greet them and exclaim over Hilary, and before Roxie had a chance to put her car away in the garage Hank drove up with Ryan.

As Hank got out of the Lincoln, Hilary raced across the gravel driveway toward him. "Daddy, Daddy, see how beautiful I am now."

Roxie noticed the flash of incredulous surprise and delight on Hank's face and felt pleased with herself for helping to put it there. He swung Hilary up in his arms and smiled at her. "You've always been beautiful."

"No, I haven't. But I am now. Georgia did it."

"Well, good for Georgia."

"You sure look different, Hil," Ryan said as he came around to Hank's side of the car.

"But good, huh, Ryan? Don't I look good?"

"Yeah, I guess so. You look good with short hair."

"I know." Hilary beamed at everyone standing in the driveway. "Now I want to get down, Daddy, so I can see Como before we leave for Grandpa and Grandma's house."

"I want to see Como, too, Dad," Ryan added.

Charlie stepped forward. "I'd be delighted to take them back to the corral. I imagine Como would enjoy a visit with them, as well."

"Fine." Hank lowered his daughter to the ground and Charlie escorted the children around to the side patio gate.

When they were gone, Hank walked over to Roxie and rested his hands on her shoulders. "Thanks. Obviously your plan worked like a charm."

"There were moments I was scared to death."

"Scared? It was only hair." He grinned. "I was prepared for the worst."

"You can say that, now that everything turned out fine. Besides, you're the parent. I'm not."

He looked deep into her eyes. "For not being the parent, you did a hell of a job with this mess."

"I—thanks." She flushed with pleasure.

His grip tightened. "And now that the hair business is over, I can hardly wait to drop these kids off at their grandparents' house and come back to pick you up. Are you packed?"

"Just about."

"Great." He squeezed her shoulders. "Why don't you finish whatever you have to do? I'll drag them away from Charlie and Como and be back in less than half an hour."

"Okay."

He released her and started toward the patio gate. "Oh, and Roxie?" he said, turning around.

"Yes?"

"Don't overpack." He smiled. "The emphasis this weekend won't be on clothes."

"Oh?" She arched her eyebrows. "What will the emphasis be?"

"Lady, if you don't know, then I haven't been doing my job." He started back toward her. "I think a reminder is in order."

"That's okay," Roxie said, hurrying toward the front door as she imagined the neighbors with their noses pressed to their living room windows. "I understand everything perfectly."

Hank paused. "You're sure?"

"Positive. I'll pack a toothbrush and a smile."

"That's my girl." Hank winked and turned back toward the patio gate.

Half an hour later Roxie and an exceedingly small overnight bag were tucked into Hank's Lincoln. She'd left Charlie some homemade chili and Hank's phone number, in case any emergencies arose, which Charlie assured her wouldn't happen.

A light rain dampened the windshield as they drove. "Ah," Hank said, lacing his fingers through Roxie's. "Rain, just as I ordered. Nothing like a rainy day for getting cozy."

"I used to hate rainy days in Newark, but rain is so scarce here, that my whole perspective on it has changed."

"The only time I mind it is when we're behind on a construction job, but the weather's so constant in Tucson that I've almost forgotten what it's like to plan around it. The sun usually shines and we usually work."

"Except when it snows," Roxie said, glancing at him fondly.

"Yeah." Hank chuckled.

"Do you realize that if it hadn't snowed this year, we might never have met? I might not have asked Charlie to stay in the guest house, and he wouldn't have spotted you standing on the roof beam, directing your crew in a blizzard."

"Slight exaggeration. We had snow flurries. Blizzards happen in South Dakota, where I was born."

"And Newark, where I was born. Anyway, Charlie thought you made a magnificent picture standing up there."

Hank laughed. "Magnificent, huh?" He glanced at her. "And logical Roxie probably wondered who that damn fool was who didn't have sense enough to come in out of the snow."

"The truth is," she said softly, "that I thought you were magnificent, too."

"Oh, yeah?"

"You ought to know by now that I don't use the logical part of me when I respond to you."

Hank sighed deeply. "Honey, I sure love whatever part you use."

"That sounded pretty suggestive."

"It *was* pretty suggestive. This has been one long morning. Poor Ryan didn't get much in the way of batting practice because I kept staring off into space when I was supposed to be pitching him the ball." He turned down a quiet street lined with sidewalks.

The tidy homes, some one-story ranch-styles and some split-level, were set on average sized lots. Bicycles leaned in carports and basketball hoops hung above them. The steady rain kept the children inside, but Roxie imagined that a usual Saturday afternoon would find the neighbors working in their yards and the kids wheeling around on their bikes or playing touch football in someone's front yard. Several people had planted grass, and unless she looked at the mountains, Roxie might imagine that she was back in Newark.

"This is it," Hank announced, pulling into the driveway of a split-level frame house painted desert tan. His landscaping of low-water, desert plants was more imaginative than that of his neighbors, and he'd turned his carport into an enclosed garage, but otherwise the architecture was similar to the rest of the block and fairly ordinary.

"Very nice, Hank," Roxie said, wondering if she could be looking at her future home. Without meaning to, she contrasted it to the house nestled in the mesquite trees where Hank had taken her on Thursday night. Feeling traitorous, she admitted to herself that she liked the other one better. But a house didn't matter, she decided. People mattered.

"Needless to say this isn't my dream home," Hank explained as he reached for the automatic garage door opener in the glove compartment. "Sybil and I had planned to move, and then she died. I couldn't uproot the kids at that point, and I'd lost the heart for it, anyway." He pushed a button and the double garage door slid up. He pulled in next to his truck and switched off the engine as the door closed behind them.

"Hank, it's a very nice house. Don't apologize. Once I leave my plush situation at the Osborns, I'll be lucky to afford a town house big enough for both me and Charlie."

He glanced at her. "Charlie? You're planning to take care of him even after you leave the Osborns?"

"Yes," she said, looking directly at him. "I won't have him on the street again."

Hank seemed to think about that for a moment before nodding in agreement. "That's fine," he said, reaching over the back seat for her overnight bag.

Roxie smiled. They'd just settled something without even talking about it. Hank had accepted the idea that if Roxie agreed to marry him, Charlie was part of the bargain. If Hank was so easy to convince on that point, then the idea of a baby shouldn't throw him, either. Roxie looked forward to a wonderful weekend.

Hank helped her out of the car and ushered her in through a door that led to a spotless kitchen in a blue-and-white country decor. It was tasteful and welcoming, but Roxie had the urge to pull down the curtains patterned with cows and geese and replace them with Mexican serapes. The Osborns focused on Oriental design and here she found the atmosphere of a farm house. Roxie wondered if anyone in Tucson liked the Southwestern look that she found so appealing.

"What do you think?"

She turned to find Hank watching her. "Honestly?"

"Honestly." He set her overnight bag on a kitchen stool.

She met the assessing look in his clear gray eyes and knew that she couldn't fool him into believing that she felt at home here. She was in another woman's house, confronted with another woman's tastes. He must have seen that as quickly as she had.

But as she studied his face and wondered how to answer his question, the importance of the decorating scheme faded. Who cared what a room looked like when it contained this man? She'd never seen anyone look better in old clothes, and her gaze roamed lovingly over his often-washed jeans and his Craddock Construction T-shirt under a faded, partially unzipped jacket. Heaven was being held in his arms. Slowly she took off her coat and walked over to him. "I think," she said, "that it's been a very long time since you kissed me."

"An eternity," he agreed, wrapping his arms around her. "I should have my head examined for leaving you unkissed for so long."

She snuggled against him and gazed up into his face. "Just don't ever let it happen again."

"Don't worry." His mouth moved hungrily over hers.

At once she was on fire for him. She found the tab on his jacket zipper and put an inch of space between them in order to pull it down. Once the jacket was pushed aside she molded her aching breasts against the soft cotton of his T-shirt.

His mild exercise with his son earlier in the day had given him the faint aroma of male sweat, and she breathed in his scent gratefully. This was what she needed, to press her body against Hank's and feel his desire swelling between them. Nothing mattered but being with him like this and communicating her passion with the urgent pressure of her lips and the whispering touch of her fingers.

She stroked the side of his neck and followed the curve of his ear with a feathery caress. As his tongue thrust into her mouth she buried her fingers in his wavy hair and slackened her jaw, daring him to plunge deeper. The fierceness of his response excited her. He ravished her mouth with a thoroughness that left her heart pounding.

Finally he lifted his head, and when he spoke his voice was rough with desire. "I've never loved you in the daylight."

"No."

"I think I'll like it very much."

"So will I."

He led her to the master bedroom and threw his jacket on a chair. The covers were turned back on the bed, awaiting her arrival, their lovemaking. She was pulsing with her need for him as he unbuttoned her cotton blouse and tossed it on the chair with his jacket. Then he tenderly unhooked her bra and drew it away from her shoulders.

"I'm jealous of that piece of lace," he murmured, cupping his hands where the bra had been.

She covered his hands with hers and pressed inward. "Don't be," she whispered. "You know I'd rather have you holding me."

"I want more than holding."

"You can have...anything you want." She arched her back as he lowered his head and took one dusky nipple into his mouth. The warmth of his lips made her close her eyes with pleasure; the flick of his tongue against the hard bud made her moan with desire.

Dimly she realized that he'd unfastened her slacks, but she was obsessed with the moist pressure of his mouth at her breast and the soft sounds made by his lips against her flesh. Her slacks dropped to the floor and he slipped his hand beneath the front elastic of her panties.

"Oh," she cried when he touched her, and her knees nearly buckled. Never had she craved a man's caress so much. She pushed against his gentle stroking, shameless in her desire for more. When he stopped she cried out again, but he had only paused to slide his arm behind the backs of her knees and carry her to the bed.

Her slacks fell away as he picked her up. After he settled her against the fresh sheets he pulled off her shoes and then her panties. Then, in the uncompromising daylight, he studied her, and she flushed at the intensity of his gaze. "You're embarrassing me," she murmured.

"I don't mean to," he said softly, sitting beside her and touching her cheek with the back of his hand. "You're so beautiful, and I've never had full light and the time to enjoy how beautiful you are."

"But you're so...exacting."

He smiled. "With buildings, not with people." He caressed the weight of her breast. "But even an exacting man would find joy in looking at you."

She answered his smile. "Good construction?"

"Outstanding construction."

She slipped her hand beneath his T-shirt. "Take this off," she whispered. "Take everything off. I want to look at you, too."

He grasped the back of the T-shirt in both hands and pulled it over his head. Then he stood and unfastened the metal button at the waistband of his jeans. He stripped down for her with a lack of self-consciousness that she found amazing. And he let her look.

For the first time she noticed the swirling patterns of his red-brown chest hair and a mole beneath his rib cage. She memorized his flat stomach, the indentation of his navel, and the darker hair below. He stood unabashed and allowed her to see the obvious thrust of his manhood that announced eloquently the aroused state of his body.

Slowly he walked to the bed and laid down beside her.

"No secrets now," he said, stroking the upward tilt of her breast. "You can see just how much I want you."

"Yes." She reached down, wanting to hold this part of him that fit so wonderfully inside her and brought her to such heights of pleasure. "You are beautiful, too," she said, wrapping her fingers around him.

"Roxie..." He closed his eyes briefly. "That feels very good, Roxie," he said, as his breathing grew shallow.

"You have given me so much," she murmured. "Now it's my turn." She ran her tongue over her lips.

His gray eyes grew smoky with passion as he guessed what she meant.

"But I'm an amateur," she added softly, bending down to caress him with a lingering kiss.

He quivered under her touch. "There's...no such thing," he said, and gasped as she took him into her mouth.

Roxie had never wanted this with any man, but she wanted it with Hank. Loving him completely, every bit of him, was the most natural thing in the world. Her body sang in tune with his sighs and moans of pleasure, the pleasure she was providing.

He tangled his fingers in her hair and at last tugged her gently away. "Stop," he said in a husky tone. "Please. I want—" He finished the sentence by rolling her to her back and moving over her. "This."

She had never felt so open, so free of barriers as now, when he entered her. When they were joined she moved without thought, as effortlessly as breathing, as sure of his body as hers. All awkwardness was swept away on the crest of their love, leaving them graceful as dolphins on an azure sea.

Their climax was sure and swift, the end to a dance with no missteps. It left her weeping with joy.

"Hush," he crooned, kissing her salty tears. "It's all right. Hush now, love."

"So beautiful," she sobbed. "We're so beautiful together."

"Yes." He kissed her trembling lips.

"I don't want to waste that beauty," she said, tears still wet on her cheeks.

"Waste? Nothing's wasted, Roxie. We're going to love each other for a long, long time."

"I know, but I want—" She took a ragged breath. "I want to have your baby."

He became completely still. After a moment he gazed down at her. "I can't give you that."

"The operation...could be reversed."

His silence pushed between them, a gray intrusion upon their joy. "There are no guarantees on that, Roxie," he said with careful emphasis. "The doctors made the situation clear when I had it done."

"At least we'd have a chance," she said, her gaze pleading. "I have a strong feeling that a new operation would be successful."

He closed his eyes and leaned his forehead against hers. "Oh, Roxie, don't ask this of me."

She wrapped her arms around him. "I...understand if you don't want to face another operation, but—"

"It's not that. The procedure is no big deal, really."

"Then—?" The rest of her question was understood and she waited nervously for an answer.

Hank sighed. "We could try reversing the operation if I wanted." He paused for a long, agonizing moment. "But the fact is, I don't want to."

11

DESPAIR CREPT THROUGH Roxie and drove away the warmth of loving Hank. "You don't want to try reversing the operation?" she asked, hoping she'd misunderstood.

"No, I don't." Hank rolled to his back and stared up at the ceiling. "When I made the decision in the first place, I took all things into account. A logical person like you would have been proud of me, Roxie."

"Like what? What did you take into account?"

"Oh, the things they tell you to consider, such as the possibility that one or both of your children might die and you'd want more. I decided not to borrow trouble on that one. And I imagined this situation we're in, believe it or not. I wondered what would happen if I should lose Sybil and decided to remarry. Would I want to have another child with this new wife? The answer was no. It still is."

"I don't understand," Roxie said woodenly. "How could you decide something like that?"

"It's simple. I have two children, and that's plenty in this day and age, with the cost of everything from orthodontia to college. Besides that, I've been through diapers and 2:00 a.m. feedings, and colic and chicken pox. Ryan and Hilary are becoming more self-sufficient every day and I wouldn't relish going back to the days of a dependent little baby."

"Not even—" She paused to swallow the lump in her throat. "Not even if you knew how much it would mean to me?"

"Roxie, listen." He raised up and turned on his side, propping his head on his hand. "If you marry me, and I hope to God you do, you'll have your hands full with Hilary and Ryan. And you've barely gotten to know them, to love them. We'll spend more time together, the four of us. You'll see how complete a life we'll already have. We don't need a baby."

"*We* don't? How can you speak for me?" Her despair curdled into anger. "You've had your chance to hold a newborn child. You've seen their first tooth and heard their first word. Don't you understand? I want that chance, too."

"You paint a wonderful picture of parenting, but don't forget the constant demands of a tiny baby, the feeding, the dressing, the changing. You're right—I have been through it, and it's a lot of work."

"I would love every minute of that work, because the baby would be ours, Hank. Don't you want to have our child?"

He tucked his arm around her waist and drew her close. "I want you, Roxie. Children are a temporary thing, but marriage, if you're lucky, is forever. I know part of what I'm saying is selfish, but Ryan and Hilary are finally at the stage where they can spend the night away from home, like this weekend. Before too much longer we'll be free of the constant responsibility children bring. A baby means starting all over again."

She stiffened in his arms. "Maybe that's what I want, starting over. Maybe I don't want to move into your ready-made niche and become your carefree playmate."

"Roxie, you're twisting my words. I don't want you in a niche at all; that's my point. Sybil and I were bogged down with the responsibilities of family, but you and I have a chance to escape that, to have an exciting love affair that isn't interrupted by the almost constant needs of a young child."

"I can see that's what you want," Roxie said, moving out of his embrace and leaving his bed. "Obviously I misjudged the situation. I thought the only thing standing in the way of our having a baby was an operation that you had before you knew me."

"I don't make decisions lightly. Perhaps the way I've responded to you, the speed with which I asked you to marry me, led you to believe otherwise. I knew exactly what I was doing when I had a vasectomy, just as I know exactly what I'm doing in asking you to be my wife."

"Wife?" She reached for her clothes. "I don't think you really want a wife, Hank. You had one of those, and she was uninteresting after a while because she became a mother and couldn't tend to your needs always. Maybe what you want is a...a concubine."

"Roxie!" He swung his legs out of bed and stood beside her, magnificent in his nakedness and his anger as he gripped her arm. "That's a rotten thing to say."

She steeled herself against the appeal of his virility. "Perhaps, but logic tells me I'm right."

"Damn your logic!" He grasped her other arm and pulled her to face him. "I love you, and I don't want to watch you work yourself to death with the two kids I already have and another one, as well. You have no idea how the pressure could kill your spirit, but I do."

She glared up at him. "I believe you underestimate the strength of my spirit. I'm not a coward."

"Neither am I!" he thundered. "Just more knowledgeable and realistic than you, because I've had more experience. Making the adjustment with Hilary and Ryan will drain us enough without adding the complication of a baby."

"I have a feeling," she began, fighting back tears, "that no adjustments will be necessary."

"Roxie, don't crucify us on this issue."

"Why not?" Tears leaked from the corners of her eyes. "Why should we go on, when I know how much a baby means to me and you have no intention of having another one? We'll only create more pain, because the problem won't go away, Hank."

"I think it might," he said gently. "Once you have a chance to know my kids."

"No." She shook her head. "That's what you hope will happen, but it won't. I want this baby."

"More than me?"

His image blurred as tears flooded her eyes. "I don't know. Maybe—maybe I do," she choked out.

"I can't believe—" Hank's sentence was interrupted by the ringing of the bedside phone. He released his grip on her arms and frowned, as if wondering what the noise could be.

"Answer it, please," Roxie said, buttoning her blouse with shaking fingers. "This discussion is over, anyway."

He glanced at her once more before walking over to the telephone and picking up the receiver. He spoke to the person briefly and turned. "It's Charlie. He wants to talk to you."

Roxie stared at the receiver in Hank's hand. Charlie was the last person she wanted to hear from right now. Most of this mess was his doing.

"You'd better take it," Hank said, holding out the receiver. "He sounds upset."

Join the group, Roxie thought. Reluctantly she took the receiver from Hank. "Charlie? Is something wrong?"

"Oh, Roxie, my child, I feel dreadful about this, just

dreadful. You were right; I should have rested on my laurels once I brought you and Hank together."

"Charlie, what is it?" Alarm swept through her like a brush fire.

"It's Como. She's...gone."

"Gone? How could she be gone?"

"It's all my fault, entirely my fault. I took her for a walk after we'd finished reading some lovely sonnets, and she wanted to travel west, you see, so we did, and—oh, Roxie, I'm so sorry."

"Charlie," Roxie said, barely able to whisper the words. "Charlie, she's not dead, is she?"

"No, goodness no. At least not the last time I saw her."

"Then where is she?"

"I don't know," Charlie wailed. "I tried to keep up with her after she pulled the lead rope out of my hand, but she's very fast, Roxie. Then, when I lost sight of her completely, I went back to the house and found the keys to your car."

"Oh, my God."

"Don't fret. It's only a small dent. Can't be seen from the other side at all. But the Osborns' mailbox is a casualty, I'm afraid. And the deputy would have taken away my license for driving on the wrong side of the road, except that I didn't have one, you see. He's here with me now, Deputy Grundy. Would you like to speak with him?"

"No, I mean, yes, but face-to-face. Where are you? Have they arrested you, Charlie?"

"No, I don't believe I'm under arrest. I'm standing in the kitchen. Deputy Grundy brought me home in his patrol car, because, you see, I wasn't allowed to drive your car anymore."

"I'll be right there, Charlie. Don't move."

"Deputy Grundy said I had to stay here, too, until you

came back. Roxie, I wouldn't have disturbed your weekend for the world. I hope that you and Hank—"

"Never mind," Roxie said, cutting him off. "I'll be there immediately."

"All right, Roxie. So very sorry, my dear."

Roxie dropped the receiver into its cradle and turned to Hank, who was already nearly dressed. "You'll have to take me home right away. Como's escaped; Charlie tried to drive my car, and he got picked up by the police."

"Good God."

Roxie put on her shoes and left the room. "Hurry," she urged over her shoulder.

Hank soon followed, pulling on his jacket as he entered the kitchen. Roxie stood by the door in her coat with her overnight bag in her hand. He glanced at the bag. "You're not coming back, then?"

"No, I'm not, Hank. I have to straighten this mess out, anyway."

"Maybe it won't take long. I'll help."

"That's not necessary. I'm sure that you have other things to—"

"Be quiet, Roxie. If you want to take the overnight bag with you, that's fine, but I'll help you with Charlie and we'll hunt for Como together. Look at it logically," he said with a sad smile. "The more people who help you look, the sooner you'll find that llama."

"You're right, of course. I appreciate your concern."

He took his keys from a peg by the door. "Cut the polite talk, Roxie," he said, ushering her into the garage. "I'd rather have you yelling at me than giving me courteous little speeches."

"Then perhaps I'd better say nothing at all."

"Perhaps."

They rode back to the Osborns in silence. The rain had

stopped, which probably explained Charlie's decision to take Como for a walk, Roxie concluded. He'd wanted to exercise the llama while he had the chance.

The Pima County Sheriff's Department patrol car sat conspicuously in front of the house, not far from the crushed mailbox. Roxie decided Charlie must have knocked down the mailbox and then run over it. She should be grateful, she supposed, that he hadn't killed someone. The thought of Charlie behind the wheel of her car paralyzed her with fear. He must have been desperate if he'd tried such a thing.

As soon as Hank stopped the car Roxie jumped out and ran toward the house. She found Charlie and Officer Grundy in the kitchen, each of them perched on a kitchen chair eyeing the other warily. They both stood when she rushed into the room.

"Miss Lowell?" The deputy was thin and nervous, with a neat mustache designed, she decided, to make him look older. He couldn't have been much more than twenty-two. "Are you acquainted with this man?" the deputy asked.

"Yes, I certainly am."

"Are you aware that he has no valid driver's license, and apparently no driving experience?"

"Yes, Deputy Grundy, I am. I apologize for all of this. Charlie panicked when the llama escaped, and didn't want to bother me while I was...away." She heard Hank's footsteps behind her and the slight clearing of his throat. "His intentions were honorable, I'm sure."

"Where is the car?" Hank asked.

"About three blocks from here," Deputy Grundy replied. "Fortunately he didn't get far before I spotted him sailing along in the wrong lane. Cars were dodging him left and right, but nobody hit him."

"Thank the Lord," Roxie murmured.

"We left your vehicle parked and locked, Miss Lowell," the deputy said, obviously proud of saving the day. "But there appears to be a fresh dent in the left side. I need to know if you want to press charges, since Mr. Hartman obviously didn't have your permission to drive the car."

"Heavens no," Roxie said, shocked at the idea.

"Then we'll have just the two citations," Deputy Grundy said, reaching for a notebook in his back pocket. "Assuming that you have proof of insurance, Miss Lowell."

"Yes, I do. What—what sort of fines are we talking about?"

"Well, driving on the wrong side of the road will cost him about sixty-five, and driving without a valid license is another forty. Is that insurance form in your car?"

"Yes, but I have a copy in my bedroom," Roxie said, mentally kissing a chunk of her savings account goodbye. She was impatient to finish with the legalities of Charlie's driving escapade so they could concentrate on finding Como. But where would they look?

"I'll pay the fines, Roxie," Hank said as she started to leave the room. "And replace the mailbox."

She turned. "Don't be ridiculous. Charlie is my responsibility."

"Yes, but if it hadn't been for me, none of this would have happened."

"We'll discuss it later," she said, clenching her teeth. She glanced at Charlie, who was looking from her face to Hank's with a worried expression on his face. He knew, she thought as she left the kitchen, that she and Hank were no longer on good terms with each other.

She returned quickly with the insurance form and handed it to the deputy. "I understand that we must take care of this first," she said, "but my primary concern is finding the llama that escaped. Can you help at all?"

The deputy tore the tickets from his book and directed Charlie to sign them. "I'll get on the radio and alert the officers in the area, ma'am," he said as he waited for Charlie to sign both citations, "but I can't promise it'll be a top priority." He took a second notepad from his breast pocket and clicked his ballpoint pen. "Could you describe this animal?"

Charlie finished signing the tickets and stepped forward. "She has sensitive brown eyes and she appreciates good sonnets. She's very good-natured, and if she weren't in love she wouldn't have—"

"Just a minute, sir," Deputy Grundy tapped on his notebook with the pen and glanced in mute appeal toward Roxie. "Color?"

"White," she said quickly. "Adult female llama who goes by the name of Como. A llama looks a bit like a camel without a hump. They—"

Deputy Grundy held up his hand. "I do know what a llama looks like. I've been to the zoo. And she was headed in which direction?"

"West," Charlie answered immediately, "and I'm convinced that her true love is in that direction. For days now she's been pining away, and I thought perhaps—"

"True love?" Deputy Grundy stopped making notes and looked at Roxie with an expression that told her he was doubtful of Charlie's sanity.

"She's in season, deputy," Roxie explained quietly.

"Oh." The young man colored. "Well, uh, I'll put it on the radio, like I said, but I'd advise you folks to begin a search immediately, maybe call the radio and TV stations. We can't spend much time on lost animals." He tore out Charlie's copy of each ticket and handed it to him. "No more driving, Mr. Hartman, unless you take lessons and are issued a license."

Charlie drew himself up and spoke with dignity. "Young man, I never intend to sit behind the wheel of a vehicle like that again, at least not until they improve the steering mechanisms. There's far too much room for error."

"Yes, sir." The deputy bit his lip and exited quickly.

"Well," Roxie said when he had gone. "What next? I agree that we should call the TV and radio stations, but how can we organize a search most efficiently?"

"I think someone should stay here, in case a call comes in that Como was located," Hank said, thinking out loud. "Whoever is out searching can check back periodically, to find out if—wait, that's the answer, the mobile phone in my truck. I'll take the car home and bring the truck back. We'll search in that."

"Good." Roxie pushed aside her personal confusion regarding Hank and their relationship. The important issue now was finding Como, and Hank had an excellent idea. "While you're gone, Charlie and I will call the stations and the animal shelters. When you get back I'll go with you in the truck, and Charlie can stay by the telephone."

"Right. I won't be long." Hank turned and sprinted out the front door. Roxie heard the car leave in a spurt of gravel.

Charlie touched her arm. "Roxie, I can't tell you how—"

"No, Charlie, you can't," she said, grabbing the telephone book and thumbing through it. "We have far too much to do for you to tell me anything. Later we'll talk."

"You're right, of course," Charlie said contritely. "Read me the numbers and I'll make the calls."

"All right. Here's the first one." Roxie rattled off the number and Charlie dialed. While he talked she found a pad of paper and wrote down the numbers for the other radio and television stations and for the animal shelters. "Here," she said, thrusting the pad at Charlie. "I'm going to look for Fran's address book, although I'm afraid she took it to China with her. One of her friends here in town might know where they tried to breed Como the first time."

"Excellent thinking, Roxie." Charlie began dialing the next number on the list.

A thorough search of the study turned up one old book of addresses and telephone numbers, but Roxie feared it wasn't current. Still, it was all she had. By the time she returned to the kitchen, Charlie was half-finished with the first list of numbers.

"Are the stations going to help?" she asked as he hung up from another call.

"Oh, my, yes. Such lovely people. One disc jockey said he'd open a 'loose llama line' exclusively for people to report whether they've seen Como."

"I hope it helps. I hope we find her." Roxie paced the length of the kitchen. "I know she cost the Osborns a lot of money, but that's not the real problem. They love her as if she were their child or something. If anything happens to Como, they'll never forgive me, or trust me again."

"Roxie, you mustn't say that. I'm the one to blame for this, not you." The burden of guilt had thoroughly quenched his usual sparkle.

Roxie cursed herself for expecting too much of Charlie and placing him in this position. "No, Charlie, you're not to blame. I'm the one who saddled you with the responsibility. I shouldn't have."

"But I wanted you and Hank to have time alone," he protested, wringing his hands. "It was part of the plan."

Roxie sighed. "Never mind, Charlie. Just keep calling. When you've finished with those numbers, I have this book with some of the Osborns' friends listed. You can try them all and find out if anyone knows where they took Como to be bred. And the vet. Maybe he has information about it."

Charlie's lined face looked older than ever before. "We simply must find her," he said, dialing the next radio station.

Hank arrived shortly after that. They left Charlie with the number of the truck's mobile telephone in case he discovered through his calls where Como might be, and they also promised to call Charlie immediately if they found the llama.

"According to Charlie, the last time he saw her she was headed west on Sunrise Drive, right?" Hank asked Roxie as they drove away from the house.

"Yes. I hope she didn't stay on it, though. The traffic is—" She couldn't finish the sentence as a picture of Como dodging Saturday-afternoon traffic flashed into her mind. The llama wouldn't survive long with cars zooming by at forty-five miles an hour.

"First of all, we've got to give her credit for some sense," Hank said. "We'll assume she turned off on a side street and continued west that way. She may have left the streets altogether, you know, to travel across the golf course."

"Oh, I hope so. Except that, if she's done that she might follow one of the washes up into the mountains. And then—"

"Don't think about that," Hank said, shifting down so they could take the drive at a slow enough pace to look for any signs of Como. "She hasn't been gone long, and someone is bound to have seen her. A loose llama will attract attention, believe me."

"I guess so." Roxie tried to follow Hank's advice and not imagine the dangers Como would face if she became lost in the mountains. But what chance would she have against a pack of hungry coyotes? Their food supply was reduced this time of year and Como, tame as she was, would be easy prey. Besides coyotes there were mountain lions, or she might startle a rattler in hibernation and be bitten.

"What we have to do is think like a llama," Hank said. "If you were Como, and you wanted to travel west, but the way was filled with speeding cars, what would you do?"

"Hank, I can't think like a llama. I'm having trouble thinking at all because I'm so worried."

"Come on, Roxie. Use that logical mind of yours. Between your logic and my intuition, we'll find her, but we have to work at it."

"Okay, I'll try." Roxie examined the street they were traveling and tried to picture herself on foot and frightened. "First of all, if she turned off it would have been to the right. I can't believe she'd cross traffic."

"I agree, but where?"

"I don't know. We've already passed some streets where she might have done that, although they didn't look like the sort that would invite her to—wait, Hank, there! The entrance to that exclusive development, with all the flowers and the waterfall. She might have been attracted by the waterfall, don't you think? She could be thirsty by now."

"It's an idea. Maybe the guard at the gate has seen something."

"And Hank, the golf course is right here, too. If I were Como, I'd have turned off at this place."

"See?" He grinned at her. "I knew you could do it."

"We have no idea if I'm right, yet." She resisted the appeal of that grin with everything she had in her. They were cooperating on this search because it made logical sense to do so. Once they'd found Como, and she prayed they would, their time together would be at an end.

The guard at the gate became very excited when they mentioned a white llama. "So that's what it was? I saw this animal come trotting in here as if it owned the place. When it stopped to drink at the waterfall I tried to catch it, but I didn't have any luck. It had on a halter with a rope dangling from it."

"Hank, she's here!" Roxie clutched the dashboard of the truck.

"Well, ma'am, she was here," the guard said, "but she took off across the golf course. I called the pro shop and told them about it. They don't want animals on the course, you know. Bad for the greens and all."

"Can we get on that course?" Hank asked.

"Not supposed to. It's private, you know."

"This llama is an extremely valuable animal," Hank persisted. "We'd pay whatever fee necessary to rent a golf cart so that we could look for her."

"Well, sir, a club membership is several thousand dollars."

Hank glanced at Roxie and rolled his eyes. "Surely there's another way," he said to the guard.

The guard brightened. "You could pay for a night at the resort. Resort guests have golfing privileges. You could rent a cart then."

Hank sighed and shook his head. "We'll use that plan if necessary, but I'd rather deal with this more directly. Could I use your telephone to call the pro shop, please? Perhaps something can be worked out."

The guard thought about the request for a moment. "Yeah, I guess that'd be all right," he said finally.

Roxie waited impatiently while Hank talked on the phone. She heard him laughing and talking with the pro shop manager as if they were old friends, and soon he was back.

"Well?" she asked, as he drove through the entrance and made a U-turn so they could leave.

"We can have a cart, but we aren't supposed to interfere with play."

"That's wonderful! How did you convince him?"

Hank glanced at her. "I told him that I'd bought this expensive white llama for my wife as a wedding present and I'd accidentally left the gate open and the damned thing ran away the first day. I mentioned that if I didn't get that llama back, my wife had threatened to sleep in the guest room for the next forty years. It seems that most people want to smooth the rocky path of true love."

Roxie stared at him. "My Lord, you sound like Charlie."

"I told you before that Charlie and I understand each other."

"Then perhaps you ought to know that Charlie was the one who looked up the information about reversing your operation. Essentially that was his idea."

Hank's jaw clenched. "So the old guy's not perfect. Have you noticed that he never talks about a family of his own? I'd guess he's never had one, and unless he's changed a diaper, he's not qualified to give advice about having babies."

"I think," said Roxie, "that he was giving advice about the compromises that could be made, if people truly love each other."

Hank stopped in front of the pro shop and turned off the motor. "That works both ways," he said, and opened the truck door. "Coming?"

"Yes." Roxie jerked open her own door. "And I'm driving the cart."

"Suit yourself."

Roxie had never driven an electric golf cart before, and she learned that the lightweight vehicle gained considerable momentum on the downward slopes of the golf path.

Hank clutched the pole supporting the cart's canopy as

they came within inches of smashing into the back of another cart at the bottom of a steep hill. "Ever done this before?" he asked mildly as she maneuvered around the other cart and continued down the path until she was even with a man lining up his shot.

"Dozens of times," she muttered. "Hey, sir!" she called to the lone golfer.

"Roxie, the man was in the middle of his swing," Hank said and winced as the golf ball skittered off the trunk of a nearby tree and the golfer swore eloquently.

"Sir, have you seen a white llama around?" Roxie shouted across the fairway.

The man turned toward them and leaned on his golf club. "Sure," he called back. "And two pink elephants and a purple zebra. Now would you mind terribly if I continued my game, or shall we elaborate on this zoological discussion?"

"A white llama, about so high," Roxie continued, desperate for information. "Please, she was last seen on this golf course and we have to find her."

"No, I haven't seen a white llama, but I'll give you some advice, young lady. This is a very difficult course, with a lot of natural hazards. Don't make yourself one of them, okay?"

"Okay. Sorry." Subdued, Roxie drove down the path. "I'm just so worried about Como," she said to Hank.

"I know. Just wait until people have finished knocking the little white ball wherever they're knocking it, and you'll be fine."

"I don't know the first thing about golf."

"I figured as much. Want me to drive the cart for a while?"

"No. I think I've about got the hang of driving now, and doing something makes me feel better. Ever since I heard about Como I've felt so helpless, and I—Hank! I see a flash of white!" She whipped the golf cart to the left and gunned it as they churned across the fairway.

"Fore!" shouted a male voice.

"Roxie, duck!" Hank commanded.

She did as she was told and a golf ball ricocheted off the canopy support and landed with a plop in Hank's lap.

"Oh, great," Hank groaned as Roxie floored the accelerator and the cart jounced across the fairway. "Same guy, and now we have his golf ball. Here he comes, running after us, and he's mad as hell."

"Never mind. Just throw it out."

Hank shrugged. "Oh, well." He tossed the ball over his shoulder. "You couldn't have played it with that lie, anyway!" he shouted back at the irate man.

"Hank, it's her. She's still heading west, see?"

"Yeah, and if you take this cart much farther we'll blow all four tires on the cactus in that wash."

Roxie brought the cart to an abrupt stop. "Then I'll go on foot."

"No." Hank grasped her arm. "Not in those shoes, you don't."

"But—"

"Get a bead on her. Aren't there some houses over there where she's headed?"

"Yes, there are. Could one of those places be her destination?"

"Let's hope. Turn the cart around and we'll take it back and transfer to the truck again. I think I can find that cluster of houses."

The golfer was alongside them now. "Listen, you banana brains, what do you mean tearing across the fairway like that? And what about my shot? How can I record that one, huh? Just tell me how to score that one."

Hank smiled at him. "Sorry, Jack. We'd like to stay and discuss the finer points of the game with you, but we have a llama to catch. Step on it, Roxie."

As they whipped back to the pro shop Roxie thought of the scolding she could be getting from Hank. "I wonder if what happened could be considered interfering with play?" she asked tentatively.

"Nah. We just added some creative challenges, that's all."

"Thanks," she said. "Thanks for not landing into me. I don't know if I could take it right now."

"You seem to forget," he said softly, "that I love you."

Her heart squeezed at the statement. But did he really love her, if he wouldn't consider becoming the father of her child?

They traded the cart for the truck and started back in the direction of the cluster of houses. When the mobile phone rang, Hank picked it up and spoke briefly with Charlie.

"We're on the right track," he said to Roxie after he hung up. "Charlie's located the people with the male llama, and from the address I'd say they live somewhere in that cluster of houses."

"You're kidding."

"No, ma'am. Apparently Como knew what she wanted and went after it." Hank dialed a number on the mobile phone. "Is this Mrs. Griffith?" He paused for an answer. "That's right, we got that word from Mr. Hartman. Sure enough, we spotted Como a few minutes ago heading in your direction. When she gets there, we'd sure appreciate it if you'd tie her lead rope to something sturdy. We're on our way."

By the time they arrived at the address Charlie had given them, Mrs. Griffith was standing next to a well-tied Como and stroking her neck. Como seemed oblivious, however, as she touched noses with a handsome black llama on the opposite side of the tall rail fence.

"Will you look at that," Roxie said. "Charlie was absolutely right."

"So, are you going to let the lovers share the same pen tonight?" Hank raised an eyebrow in her direction.

"No, I'm certainly not. I don't want the responsibility of a pregnant llama. Too many things could go wrong."

He stopped the truck and turned to her. "I wouldn't want to put too fine a point on this, because the analogy doesn't carry very far, but I feel much the same way about you having a baby."

Roxie opened the door of the truck. "You're right, the analogy doesn't carry very far. It's all right, Hank. You've stated your case and I have no right to question your logic. But I don't have to agree with you, and because I don't, we'd best end this relationship before we hurt each other any more. I appreciate your help in finding Como, but after we get her home, we won't be seeing each other again."

The muscles worked in his jaw. "If that's the way you want it."

"It is."

He swung down from the truck. "Then let's get this show on the road."

THE TASK OF RETURNING Como to her corral and retrieving Roxie's car took very little time. Within an hour everything was accomplished and Hank had left. Before he'd driven away he'd offered once again to pay Charlie's fines. Roxie had refused.

"She seems fine, Charlie," Roxie said later as she used a currycomb to brush burrs from Como's soft coat. "You can stop worrying now."

"She does seem to be in excellent shape, I dare say."

Charlie kept circling Como, and the llama followed him with her dark gaze. "Perhaps she'd like a spot of poetry after her adventure?"

Roxie smiled. "Perhaps."

Charlie pulled his tattered version of Shakespeare's sonnets from his coat pocket and perched his glasses on his nose. "Let me see. Here we are. 'Shall I compare thee to a summer's day?'"

As Charlie read the romantic lines, Roxie tried to block out the beautiful message in them that reminded her of loving Hank. She wasn't successful, and by the end of the sonnet she had tears in her eyes.

Charlie hastily tucked away his book and his glasses before hurrying to her side. "Roxie, my child, please tell me what's wrong," he said, putting a hand on her arm. "I know something dreadfully sad happened between you and Hank and I've been beside myself worrying. That is, when I wasn't worrying about poor Como."

Roxie looked into his kind face and nearly lost control. Determined not to cry, she began brushing Como vigorously. "I guess Hank won't be my valentine, after all," she said.

"Why ever not? You two were getting on so famously."

Roxie tried to clear the lump from her throat. "Charlie," she said tremulously, "do you consider having a baby an expression of love between two people?"

"Why, I suppose it can be, Roxie."

"What do you think of a man who refuses that experience, even when...he knows that the woman he loves wants a b-baby very much?" With a sob Roxie put her arms around Como and cried against her soft white coat.

"Oh, my dear." Charlie patted her shoulder awkwardly. "I'm so sorry. Now, now. Maybe it's not as bad as all that. Maybe Hank needs time to get used to the idea."

"Why?" Roxie wailed. "He shouldn't have to 'get used to' the idea of having a baby with me. If he loved me, he'd want to do it." She lifted her damp face and turned to him. "Wouldn't he, Charlie?"

Charlie's gaze shifted. "Well, now, Roxie—"

"He would. I know he would. And I never want to see him again!" Once more she buried her face against Como's neck, and the llama nuzzled her shoulder as if to comfort her.

"Oh, dear—oh, dear. Two love stories with sad endings." Charlie sighed. "Maybe I'm through, washed up, as they say. Maybe I've lost the old touch, the savoir faire to do this job. Retirement's been suggested, but I've never listened. I've been stubbornly clinging to my motto that Love Conquers All, but now I just don't know. I just don't know."

Toward the end of this amazing speech Roxie lifted her head and wiped her eyes. "Charlie, what on earth are you talking about? Retire from what?"

"My job, of course." He took out his handkerchief and polished the gold pin on his lapel. "Turn in my badge, so to speak. I was so certain of you and Hank. The two of you had restored my faith in the wonder of true love, dispelled my fears that love is out of fashion in this modern world. But now..." He shook his head sadly and folded his handkerchief into a neat square. "The thing of it is, I hate to end my career with a failure."

Roxie put down the currycomb and faced Charlie. "End what career? You're scaring me again with this crazy talk, Charlie."

"I guess it's time you knew." He returned the handkerchief to his pocket. "Although I hate to admit the truth now, after what's happened."

"What truth?" She eyed him with trepidation. "Who are you?"

He swept off his hat and gave her a courtly bow. "St. Valentine, in person and at your service."

12

SPEECHLESS, unable to respond to such an audacious statement, Roxie stared at him incredulously.

"Obviously you don't believe me. Well, I had hoped to tell you under happier circumstances, perhaps when you announced your marriage plans. Under those conditions you might have been more open to the concept."

"My God, you *are* crazy," she whispered.

"That's possible, after all the centuries I've been handling this assignment."

"You really do imagine that you're St. Valentine, don't you?"

"Believe me, at this moment I'd rather be good old Charlie Hartman, the down-on-his-luck chap you rescued from the park. Then I wouldn't have to accept the responsibility for this fiasco."

"How, Charlie, how are you responsible? I can't wait to hear."

He motioned to a couple of padded redwood chairs arranged near the house on an area paved with flagstone. "Perhaps we should sit down while I explain everything to you."

"Perhaps we should," Roxie said, following him out of the corral and over to the chairs. "I should probably take this sitting down, as well."

"Now, then," Charlie began when they were settled. "A long time ago, maybe in the thirteenth or fourteenth century, I hit upon the guise of a ne'er-do-well as the perfect way to move in and out of situations without being noticed. I appear, take care of my business and leave. Everyone assumes that the friendly vagabond has simply moved on. Which I have, of course, in order to bring another pair of lovers together."

Roxie shook her head. "I can't believe I'm hearing this."

"I came to Tucson this Valentine's Day for the weather," Charlie continued, unruffled by her skepticism. "That much of what I told you is true. I've a touch of arthritis in my back and the warm, dry air is immensely soothing. Had you stayed in Newark, my dear, we might not have met. I worry about those poor lovers in colder climes, and I've been thinking of training a younger assistant." He gazed morosely at the flagstone pattern beneath his feet. "Now that may not be necessary."

"An assistant," Roxie marveled. "I'd love to be there when you asked someone to take that position."

"There are those who have already asked," Charlie said with great dignity. "Geoff Chaucer for one. He was perceptive enough to notice that birds pair off on February fourteenth, and he's been fascinated with my work ever since. However, I rather favor Charles, the Duke of Orleans. Naturally you remember who he was."

"Naturally."

"What a fellow. When he sent his wife a love letter from the Tower of London on St. Valentine's Day, he started a whole new trend."

"A real trendsetter, that duke was," Roxie said, deciding to play along with this amazing fantasy. She had to give Charlie one thing, he was up on the subject of St. Valentine's Day.

"At any rate, to bring us back to the present, and you, I picked you out right away."

"Because of my name."

"Yes, and the real danger that with one wrong move you'd end up with weasel-faced Doug Kelly."

"Ah, yes, Doug." Roxie sank back in her chair. "I'll say this—whoever you are and whatever you've done, I'm grateful that you steered me away from Doug. What a mistake that would have been."

"So true. My goal was to find someone more suitable in a hurry. When I saw Hank Craddock on that roof, I believed I had my man."

"Yes, well—" Fresh tears pricked Roxie's eyes and she looked away.

"I still can't believe that I've been wrong."

"Charlie, you couldn't have foreseen this problem." Then she laughed through her tears. "Listen to me. I'm starting to sound as if I believe you. Logically speaking, you could have done all of this without being anybody but who you are, a sweet old man named Charlie Hartman."

"Some, perhaps, but not quite all. The most complicated part was the mobile telephone. Interfering with that mechanism nearly drained me of psychic energy."

"You imagine that you broke Hank's telephone that day?"

"I'm not imagining it, my dear. When I walked Como down to the construction site on St. Valentine's morning, I was determined to find some ruse to bring Hank to this house. The telephone was a bit spur-of-the-moment, but it did the trick."

Roxie gazed at Charlie for a long time. He was absolutely, totally crazy. His head was filled with incomprehensible delusions that would make a psychiatrist's day. Yet all things considered, he was a harmless old lunatic, and she still loved him. He'd been right about Doug. Her experience with Hank had taught her that she needed that wild, desperate passion to be happy. Whatever part Charlie had played in introducing her to Hank, she wasn't sorry that he had. Sad, yes. Incredibly sad. But not sorry.

Charlie shifted in his chair. "So you see, Roxie, if you and Hank are really calling it quits with each other, I may have to consider retirement."

"And then what?" Roxie wondered if he gave up being St. Valentine whether he'd find something more bizarre to keep him busy.

"I don't know." Charlie stared at his hands as they lay idly in his lap. "I've never been retired before."

"You could stay with me. You know that."

He glanced at her. "As if I really were Charlie Hartman, you mean?"

"Yes." She nodded solemnly. "As if you really were Charlie Hartman."

"I'll give it some thought, Roxie. You're a dear child for putting up with me all this time. I've caused you a lot of trouble recently."

"Fortunately the damage can be repaired," Roxie said. *Except for one broken heart*, she amended silently.

Charlie held out his lapel and peered down at the gold pin. "If I retire, I could sell this. It might be worth enough to pay for my traffic tickets, at least."

"I've always meant to ask you about that pin, Charlie. Where did you get it?"

"The pin came with the job. When I successfully complete a project, I give this pin to the lucky couple and get another. There's an endless supply of pins as long as I'm successful, but—" He paused and shrugged.

"What does the pin mean?" Roxie wondered why she was asking, as if it mattered what he said. But participating in Charlie's craziness was kind of fun. It took some of the ache from her heart.

"This is a love-knot," Charlie said, lapsing into his lecturing style. "It signifies a love without beginning and without end. This is also the sign for infinity, you know."

"Yes, I did know that much."

"And, of course, gold never tarnishes, which is why the pin is gold."

"Well, Charlie, it's lovely, but I doubt if you'll get enough for it to pay the tickets. Keep the pin. We'll dip into the money I've saved toward the down payment on a town house. We've got to fix the mailbox and the car, too."

"Yes, but what about your town house fund?"

"We have several months to get it back to the present level, which shouldn't be a problem. And I don't know about you, but I've tackled enough problems for one day."

"Quite right, my dear." He stood and straightened his bow tie. "Perhaps I'll freshen up a bit before we have dinner."

"Good idea," Roxie agreed, pushing herself from the chair with an effort. She felt as if lead weights were hanging from every joint. "Then we'll eat that chili I left you and open a bottle of wine."

"Capital."

Roxie managed to retain her composure until she was alone in her bedroom. Then she saw the piece of two-by-four with Hank's writing on it and her self-control vanished. "Why, Hank, why?" she wailed through her tears. "Why couldn't we want the same things?"

AS IT TURNED OUT, Roxie didn't have five months to restore the level of her savings. Only days after she paid Charlie's fine, the Osborns called and announced they were flying home early. They'd been thinking about Como and had found the prospect of breeding their llama more exciting than continuing their trip. They told Roxie that she was welcome to stay in the house as long as she liked, at least until she had enough saved to work out a deal on a condo or town house.

"I am moving back to the park tomorrow," Charlie announced when Roxie told him that the Osborns would return on a flight the next evening.

"Charlie, I really hate for you to do that. The Osborns won't mind if you stay a little longer, until I have the money saved and have a place for both of us."

"Absolutely not. When the Osborns return they may very well want to invite someone to use the guest house. With me there they would hesitate. I simply won't be in the way of their plans. No, it's settled. The weather is delightful now, Roxie. The bench won't be a bad place at all."

"Oh, Charlie." Roxie sighed, knowing that his decision was probably for the best. She thought the Osborns wouldn't mind having him, but she wasn't positive. Although she loved Charlie and never regretted befriending him, the Osborns might not understand her desire to take on the responsibility of an old bum from the park. "But it's only for a little while," she said. "Before the summer heat gets here, I'll manage something. I don't want you sweltering in one hundred degrees, either."

"Goodness, does it get that hot?"

"I'm afraid so. The natives say you don't mind it because the heat is dry and you don't sweat, but I think you'd notice it, Charlie. Don't worry. You'll have air-conditioned comfort by June. I promise."

"You're such a dear girl." He gazed at her with a hint of moisture in his eyes. Then he clapped his hands with determined good cheer. "We have one more evening together," he proclaimed. "I think tonight will be the night I triumph in chess."

Roxie brushed her own tears. "Think again," she said, smiling bravely.

Throughout the game she tried to ignore the depression that was settling over her and growing more dismal with every passing minute. First she had pushed Hank away, and now Charlie was leaving. Charlie had been wonderfully understanding of her moods since the miserable weekend when she and Hank had parted ways. With Charlie she didn't have to explain her silences or her sudden fits of tears. In twenty-four hours, when the Osborns arrived, she'd have to put on a cheerful facade, or face embarrassing questions.

Roxie wished that she had the money to move into a town house right away. Living here she would be forced to drive past the nursing home construction site twice each weekday and sometimes on the weekends, too. She'd hoped that with time her heart wouldn't hammer so in her chest whenever she glimpsed Hank there, but so far she seemed to be getting worse, not better.

Deliberately she allowed Charlie to win the chess game, and then they agreed that they both had work to do before the Osborns arrived. Roxie volunteered to wash all of Charlie's things one last time while Charlie tidied up the guest house. Roxie knew it wouldn't take him long; he lived immaculately.

She didn't sleep well that night, and the next morning she fed Como and scurried back inside when Charlie came out to tell the llama goodbye. Roxie didn't think she could bear to watch them together for the last time. The old man and the gentle animal had formed a special bond, and each would miss the other terribly. Charlie had made Roxie promise to read poetry to Como after he left, and Roxie secretly wondered if she'd be able to do it without bursting into tears.

Finally they were ready to leave. Charlie's battered brief-case, stuffed with everything he owned plus some nonper-ishable food Roxie had forced on him, was in the back seat of the car.

"Take a blanket, Charlie," Roxie said, rummaging through the linen closet, delaying their departure as long as possible. "It's old, and the Osborns told me to use it for pic-nics. I can get them another one."

"Thank you, but I travel light, Roxie. A blanket would weigh me down, and I won't need it, anyway."

"A pillow, then. Have the one off my bed. I can buy one today after work."

"Roxie." He touched her arm. "I don't need a pillow, ei-ther. I'll be fine as I am, as I've always been. Really."

"I just can't stand it, Charlie." She glanced at him with brimming eyes. "The thought of you, alone on a park bench tonight, is driving me crazy. Let's forget this idea. The Os-borns won't mind, and I'm sure they're not up to company so soon after a long trip, so the guest house will be free. Please, Charlie."

"No, I must be going. You'll have to trust my instincts on this, my dear. It's for the best."

She gazed into his weathered face and knew that he wouldn't change his mind. The only solution was for her to find an apartment quickly, which she was determined to do. "Then let's go, before I break down completely."

"Right," Charlie agreed, following her out the front door. "I do have one small favor to ask, however," he said as they got into the car.

"Anything, Charlie. You name it."

"Stop at the construction site and allow me to say good-bye to Hank."

Anything but that, Roxie thought, but she couldn't refuse

the old man his only request. "All right, but we haven't much time."

"I'll only be a minute."

Dutifully she pulled off the road next to the break in the cyclone fence. She saw Hank at once, as if she were equipped with radar, and in the same instant he saw her and started for the car. "Go meet him, Charlie," Roxie begged. "Don't let him come all the way over here, please."

"As you wish, my dear."

When Charlie got out of the car Hank paused and waited for Charlie to reach him. They were too far away for Roxie to hear what was said, but neither of them smiled during the short conversation. Twice Hank shook his head slowly after Charlie made some energetic motions with his hands. Roxie believed they were talking about her.

At last they shook hands and Hank clapped Charlie on the shoulder. Then Hank walked away and Charlie returned to the car. "That's it, then," he said. "Thank you."

Roxie wanted to ask what they'd said to each other, but she didn't think she had the right. Charlie didn't volunteer any information, and they rode downtown in silence. Spring was coming, Roxie noticed, thankful that Charlie wouldn't be overly uncomfortable on his park bench.

Yards were splashed with yellow and orange African daisies, and along the road blue mountain lupines blended with the yellow-blossomed brittlebush. Under other circumstances Roxie would have enjoyed this early show of color as a welcome change from Newark, which was still cold and had recently suffered through another snowstorm. But today it didn't much matter where she lived or what the weather was like. All she could see was Hank talking with Charlie. Hank shaking his head. Hank saying no. No to a baby, no to a life with Roxie, no to love.

When she parked the car in the garage, as usual, she

didn't want to get out, because then Charlie would get out, and he'd walk toward the park, except that the park would be his home now. He wouldn't come back with her to the little guest house on Calle de Suenos, street of dreams. Some dream this had turned out to be, she thought.

"Come, my dear. You'll be late for work."

With a sigh Roxie opened her door. No, she couldn't be late for work. If she lost her job, she and Charlie would be in a world of hurt. They rode the elevator together out of the parking garage to the point where she crossed the footbridge and Charlie walked to the park.

"As always, thank you for the ride," Charlie said, tipping his hat.

"Oh, Charlie." Roxie gave him a fierce hug. "I don't want you to go."

"But I'll see you soon, when I bring in the rose, and again at lunchtime."

"I know, but—"

"Don't fret, Roxie. Everything will work out, one way or another. Now chin up. I must go. I'm past my usual time at the flower shop, and I want best pick of the roses." He paused. "Of course, if I give up my position as St. Valentine, I suppose there won't be any need to continue that custom."

Roxie felt drenched in sadness. Crazy as it sounded, she wanted Charlie to keep believing that he was St. Valentine. His childlike faith in the power of true love had given him a special glow that was missing today, and Roxie wanted it back. But that was unrealistic, she reprimanded herself. Charlie had been living in a dream world, and for a short time, so had she. In the real world love was not enough to overcome life's problems.

She cleared her throat and managed a smile. "Just don't stop bringing the roses yet," she said.

"No," Charlie agreed. "Not yet."

"Goodbye, Charlie."

"Goodbye, my dear. Thank you for taking in an old fellow like me."

She shook her head but couldn't speak. He seemed to understand and tipped his hat once more before turning and walking toward the park. His pace was quick, his head up. He carried his old briefcase as if it contained a comprehensive portfolio of stocks and bonds, or the final draft of an important research project. Roxie knew that she'd never loved him more than at this moment.

13

THE RETURN OF THE OSBORNS gave Roxie something she hadn't enjoyed since leaving Newark—a trusted woman friend in whom to confide. Within two days she and Fran had become relaxed with each other, and Roxie longed for a chance to discuss Hank with the older woman. Yet because of Roxie's job they had no time alone until Saturday afternoon when Dave met some friends for golf.

Fran and Roxie had planned to spend the afternoon fertilizing and pruning the citrus trees. Fran appropriated the clippers and trimmed branches that had been nipped by frost or that dragged the ground. Roxie sprinkled red granules of fertilizer at the base of each tree and spaded them into the damp earth.

The fragrant air hung still and silent, except for the hum of bees gathering nectar from the orange and grapefruit blossoms. Even Como was gone, transferred for the week to her sweetheart's corral. Roxie had told Charlie about Como's changed status, and he was happy for the llama, but nothing, Roxie knew, could ease his disappointment concerning Hank.

As she and Fran worked, Roxie searched for a way to begin a discussion of what was bothering her. Finally she discovered her opening, and wondered why the thought hadn't occurred to her before. "You and Dave seem so happy, so in love," she said. "Even after—what is it now?"

"Twenty-six years," Fran said with a throaty chuckle. "And I have the gray hairs to prove it."

"Dave even likes the gray streaks," Roxie said, admiring Fran's short-cropped hair. "I heard him tell you not to color them."

Fran waved the clippers in the air. "Did you hear what he threatened? To get a toupee if I dyed my hair. I've never heard of anything so ridiculous."

Roxie smiled. "That's because you both like each other the way you are."

"Well, I certainly wouldn't like him with a dome doily, that's for sure."

Roxie pulled out a weed from the tree well and tossed it aside. "Fran, tell me if this is too personal, but did you ever consider…having children?"

She answered at once. "Absolutely. We wanted kids in the worst way. I couldn't have them, although we went through a truckload of military and civilian doctors before that conclusion was finally drawn."

"What about adoption?"

"We moved around too much and couldn't seem to get the paperwork together," Fran said, clipping branches as she talked. "And then, in the end, we decided to give up the whole desperate game of baby-makes-three. We considered all the things that were good about our life—our love for each other, the freedom to do as we pleased and the lack of financial burdens. We concluded that we were blessed, even without a child."

Roxie considered the implications of Fran's statements. "Any regrets?"

"None. And not for Dave, either. He could have ditched me for someone capable of providing him with a brood of little ones, but he wanted me, thank goodness." She stopped pruning and looked at Roxie. "Kids are nice, but they seldom stay around, you know. In the end, it's the person you'll be married to for the next fifty years who counts." She studied Roxie for a moment. "And now I get to ask you a personal question. Who is he?"

Roxie's mouth opened in surprise.

"Just as I thought. Are you going to tell Aunt Fran about it?"

Roxie leaned on her shovel. "Yes," she said, gazing at Fran. "I've been wanting to for days."

The story rushed out like water into a dry irrigation ditch. Roxie told everything, including the parts about Charlie and his statement about being St. Valentine, and Como's escape.

"Whew!" Fran said when Roxie had finished. "China wasn't nearly that exciting."

"I hope you're not furious that I brought Charlie here."

Fran put down her clippers and walked over to hug Roxie. "Of course I'm not furious. Would you like to ask him back? We won't be needing the guest house all summer, probably." She grinned. "Visitors don't fancy Tucson when the mercury hits a hundred and five."

"I'll certainly ask him, but I doubt if he'll come. In a way, he justified accepting my charity because he thought he was helping me find the right man. When that ran amok, I think Charlie felt useless. He's talking about 'retiring' as St. Valentine."

"My goodness." Fran chuckled. "What a sweet occupation he's created for himself."

"It is sweet, isn't it? I know he's crazy, but I like him that way. I don't want him to retire."

"Well, then." Fran eyed her shrewdly. "I suppose the only way to keep him in business is for you to patch it up with your Mr. Craddock."

"Even if it means giving up my dream of having a baby?"

"But what sort of dreams are you giving up now?"

Roxie was silent for a long time. "Quite a bit," she answered at last. "Life is pretty miserable without Hank. As I've listened to you talk about a husband being for the long run, while the kids are only temporary, I realize that it's true. I could marry some nice, boring guy who didn't excite me, just because he wanted children, and then one day the children would be gone and I'd have only him."

"That's right."

"But Fran, I yearn to have Hank's baby."

Fran sighed. "I know. Believe me, I know. But if both you and Hank aren't sold on the idea, you're looking at trouble. I can see his point. He has two children. I can also see yours."

The drone of the bees was the only sound in the sunny patio as Roxie thought about her choice. "I guess," she said at last, "that maybe I'd rather have Hank and no baby than no Hank at all."

"Maybe? This isn't the time for maybes, Roxie."

"I miss him so much." Roxie gazed at the solid comfort of the mountains. "He's all I could want in a man—kind, generous, creative, sexy..."

"Are you listening to yourself?" Fran asked.

Roxie stared at her for a long time. "I love him, Fran. More than anything or anyone else." She took a deep breath. "And I'm not letting this baby business come between us."

"That's my girl."

Roxie felt a rush of joy. Now that the decision was made to relinquish her demand for a child of her own, she couldn't imagine any other option. "Too bad I couldn't decide earlier and save everyone some grief, huh?"

Fran shook her head. "Don't be hard on yourself. You had a big expectation to give up before you could accept Hank's decision not to have any more children. Some women might never have done it."

"Only if they didn't have a man like Hank to love."

"Give me the spade," Fran said, reaching for the handle. "I think you'd better stop gardening and find that man of yours. When you have everything straightened out between the two of you, bring him around. I'd like to meet him."

Roxie hugged her. "Thanks, Fran. My mother couldn't have done a better job of advising me than you have."

"Your mother might shoot me for advising you at all. We're talking about ditching her future grandchildren, don't forget."

"Oh, I haven't." Roxie picked up a grapefruit, one of the last of the season, that had fallen from the tree. "That was part of it, of course, the idea of presenting my parents with grandchildren, but that's not the important thing, either, is it?"

"No, I don't think so."

"None of that matters if you don't have the right man."

"Go get him, Roxie."

She tossed the grapefruit in the air and caught it deftly. "I believe I will."

And she tried, but the construction crew wasn't working that day and no one answered the telephone at Hank's house. Roxie called again every half hour until ten o'clock. By then Dave had been filled in on the unfolding love story and he'd glance up from his reading each time she walked through the living room and ask if she'd reached Hank yet.

After ten she debated whether to call again and finally decided to dial the number once more at ten-thirty. Hank answered the phone.

"Roxie?" he said as soon as she spoke. "Is anything wrong?"

"No," she said, trembling at the sound of his voice. "I need to talk to you. In person."

"It's not Charlie, is it, or Como?"

"No, nothing like that. I just wondered if maybe we could...get together sometime. Sometime soon." She swallowed hard.

"Sure we can. I'd suggest right now, but the kids are asleep, and I can't leave them. Would you like to drive over?"

"Well, I—" Roxie considered the possibility and rejected it. First of all she'd be racing off to Hank's in the middle of the night, and she had no idea when she'd be back. The Osborns didn't deserve to be startled awake at four in the morning by her key in the lock. "How about tomorrow?" she suggested instead.

His reply was swift. "I'll pick you up at ten."

"What about Hilary and Ryan? Can you get someone to watch them on such short notice?"

"You let me worry about that, Roxie. Just be ready at ten."

"All right. And thank you."

There was a pause. "You know I'd walk on hot coals for a chance to be with you again, Roxie, so you don't have to thank me."

"Hank, I—" Roxie came close to blurting out her new decision and her apology for everything that had happened, but she stopped herself. What she had to say deserved being said in person. "I'll see you tomorrow at ten," she said. "Good night, Hank." Then she hung up the telephone before she was tempted to explain anything more.

By ten the next morning a warm desert wind was blowing, sweeping the sky clean of a few wispy clouds and leaving it a polished, unbroken blue. Hank arrived exactly at ten. To cover her bad case of the jitters at seeing him again, Roxie dragged him immediately into the kitchen and introduced him to Fran and Dave, who looked up from their Sunday paper with a bemused expression.

"It's wonderful to meet you," Fran said. "Would you like some coffee?"

"Thanks," Hank said, glancing at Roxie, "but we'd better be going."

"Uh, yes, we'd better," she said, waving cheerfully at Fran and Dave as they left the kitchen. "By the way, where are we going?" She glanced questioningly at Hank but he just smiled at her. The smile nearly undid her and she rushed out the front door before she made a blubbering fool of herself, fell into his arms and begged him to marry her within hearing distance of Dave and Fran.

The day was too warm for jackets. She'd worn a light-weight sweater the color of chocolate and a beige wool skirt, and Hank had on a crew-necked gray sweater and cream-colored slacks. After not being with Hank for two weeks Roxie couldn't seem to take her attention away from him.

As they drove she noticed little things that she'd missed before. The shape of his earlobe, the small mole on the curve of his cheekbone, the breadth of his hands—all were precious to her now. She hoped that he'd been telling the truth about his willingness to walk on hot coals for her. She hoped that he still loved her enough to forget her harsh words of two weeks ago.

"Did you find someone to watch the kids?" she ventured.

"Dolores came over, grumbling, but she'll stay as long as I need her to. I had to promise to take her and her boyfriend out to dinner soon, though."

"I should pay for that, considering."

"You wouldn't let me pay for Charlie's fine, so be quiet, Roxie."

She glanced at him. "Are you terribly upset with me?"

He maneuvered the Lincoln around a corner before meeting her gaze. "No," he said gently.

She sighed with relief. He didn't sound like a man who would hold a grudge. "We're going to the house, aren't we?" She recognized the route to the house his contractor friend was building, even though they'd traveled it at night before.

"Yes. No one will be there today, and he was happy to give me the key." Hank paused. "I think Ed's trying to sell me the place."

Roxie's heart began to pound as she wondered if he might seriously be considering the house, and if his decision would have anything to do with her. But he'd mentioned that it was very expensive, so perhaps she was building castles in the air. When they turned down the winding drive, she quelled the unbidden feeling of home-coming.

"Is it finished?" she asked when they stopped near the front door. The piles of scrap lumber were gone, she noticed, and the large windows, recessed into the house's thick buff walls, were sparkling clean.

"Basically it's done," Hank replied. "Ed wants to put in some low-water landscaping, but the place is about ready to go on the market."

Roxie's appreciative gaze roamed over the graceful lines of the Santa Fe-style house. Everything about it enchanted her, from the huge carved double entry doors to the round log beams that protruded from the stuccoed exterior. New leaves sprouting on the mesquite trees would soon shield the house from the sun and create a cool haven in the desert.

Engrossed in her thoughts, she didn't realize that Hank had left his seat until he opened her door and helped her out. Once she was standing beside him he dropped her hand, as if not wanting to presume too much.

He stood silently beside her, surveying the house. "Like it?" he finally asked.

"Yes," she said, afraid to admit to more.

"I put a deposit on it this morning."

Her gaze flew to his and her eyes widened.

"And if you like this house, I mean really like it, I want us to live here—you, me, Ryan, Hilary, and of course, Charlie." He paused. "And the baby."

Disoriented, she shook her head and tried to assimilate all that he'd said. "The what?" she whispered, putting her hand over her heart.

"I went to see the surgeon last week, and he's ready to try reversing the operation whenever I say."

"I can't believe this." She struggled with a light-headed feeling of unreality, of moving through a dream. "I have my little speech all ready about how I've discovered that you are more important than having a baby, and now you're telling me—"

"That I was wrong," he said, stepping forward and taking her into his arms. "I want us to have a baby, Roxie."

"Wait a minute." This might be a dream, she thought, but she'd say her piece anyway. "I don't want you to make a sacrifice that you'll regret later, just because you think that's the only way I'll be happy. It isn't. I've thought this through and spending my life with you is far more important than whether I ever have a baby."

He smiled and stroked her cheek. "That's nice to hear, but I've thought it through, too, during many unhappy nights without you. Finally I got out the old albums, the ones we put together when Ryan and Hilary were small. Looking through them, I realized those were special times. You deserve that experience, and I deserve to have it with you."

Slowly she began to believe in the moment, in what he was saying. "You really have changed your mind," she said in wonder.

"Yes."

Joy sparkled around her, rainbows reflected from the prism of this unexpected gift. "You won't be sorry when the baby cries at 2:00 a.m. and disturbs your sleep?"

"Nobody likes that part, Roxie, but when I bring that little kid into our bedroom and see the love on your face, I won't mind getting up at two in the morning."

She stared at him. Surprises were piling on top of each other. "When *you* bring the baby in?"

"You bet. I wasn't around nearly enough for the other two. I want full participation with this one. Let's schedule the baby during the slow season in construction, okay?"

Her joy overflowed and she smiled at his earnest, impractical request. "I don't think it's quite that simple."

"Sure it is. I'll get Charlie to work some of his St. Valentine's magic."

"Oh, Hank, Charlie will be thrilled with this news. He won't have to retire, after all. We have to tell him right away."

Hank pulled her close. "Maybe not right away."

"But soon," Roxie said as the friction of his body against hers transformed sparkle to languorous heat.

"Tomorrow," Hank said, kissing the curve of her neck. "We'll take him to lunch when I come downtown for the license. In the meantime, I have other plans."

"But Hank, it's broad daylight," Roxie protested, even as

she nestled closer and relished the ardor that was fueling her own.

"There are things you don't know about this house," he said, reaching beneath her sweater to rub the small of her back. "Like for instance, the master bedroom comes equipped with shutters over the window."

"How thoughtful."

"My suggestion," he said, gazing at her. "I've loved this house ever since Ed showed me the site, but I had no reason to buy it until you came along."

"And ever since we made love there, I haven't been able to imagine anyone else owning it."

"I haven't either, but we had some...problems to work out."

"I think," she said, rubbing her pelvis against his, "that we've done that."

Hank groaned. "Except for one immediate problem. Some old man once told me that I was abounding in love, and it's been frustrating keeping that bottled up the past two weeks."

"I wouldn't want you to be frustrated, Mr. Craddock."

"Good," he murmured, finding her lips and claiming the kiss that was undeniably his.

SEVERAL LONG PLEASURABLE hours later, Hank and Roxie decided that they shouldn't keep their happy secret to themselves any longer. Informing Charlie could wait until the next day, they agreed, but Hilary and Ryan deserved to be told that evening about their father's marriage plans.

They decided that Hank should break the news alone, to reduce the pressure on Hilary and Ryan and allow them to react naturally to the decision.

"What if they hate the idea?" Roxie asked as Hank drove her back to the Osborns' house.

"Then we'll deal with it," Hank replied. "But their reaction won't dictate what we do. And I doubt that they'll hate the idea, Roxie. They like you and have asked me why they haven't seen you recently."

"Yes, but that's not the same as proposing that I become their stepmother."

"Of course not." Hank squeezed her hand. "I'm not saying this will be a piece of cake, but I predict that they'll adjust pretty quickly."

"I'm scared."

"That's because you don't know Hilary and Ryan as well as I do. They'll be just fine, and you can expect that we'll all go out for spaghetti tonight to celebrate."

"But you won't force it, will you? If they'd rather not have dinner with me, I'll understand."

"No, I won't force it. And I'll call you, either way." He smiled at her. "Don't worry."

"I'll worry. Aren't you at all nervous about what they'll say?"

"Maybe a little," he said, "but it will be fine." Hank squeezed Roxie's hand again and hoped he'd convinced her. Now all he had to do was convince himself. He knew the sort of understanding that he wanted from the kids, and he prayed they were mature enough to give it to him.

He kissed Roxie at the Osborns' front door and left, feeling like a knight riding into battle for his lady love. If Ryan and Hilary objected to this marriage, he'd still go through with it, but life would be very difficult for a while.

At home he paid Dolores and sent her away with grateful thanks. Then he called Hilary and Ryan into the kitchen, their traditional powwow room.

"What's up, Dad?" Ryan asked, settling into his usual seat at the kitchen table.

"I have some news for you and Hilary," Hank replied, careful not to be cutesy and call it "good news."

"What news?" Hilary asked, leaning forward.

"I asked Roxie to marry me, and she said yes."

Both children stared at him, and Hank restrained himself from adding anything more, anything that could be construed as a bid for their approval.

"You mean, like, she'll be our mom?" Ryan asked.

"Well, yes and no, Ryan." Hank searched for the right words. "Mothers aren't objects you can replace with a new model. I'm sure Roxie would like to do some of the things with you that mothers do with their children, but she's told me herself that she wouldn't ever try to take the place of your mother."

"Is she gonna live here?" Hilary asked, twisting a lock of her short hair around one finger.

"Well, that's another thing," Hank said, realizing that he had two announcements to make, and that he was expecting a great deal of these two children. Change wasn't easy. "I've bought a new house."

"A new house? Cool!" Ryan exclaimed. "When can we go see it?"

"Whenever you want, I guess," Hank said, thrown off balance by Ryan's unexpected enthusiasm for the house. "What do you think, Hilary?"

"What's my room look like?" she asked. "Is it bigger than the one I have now?"

"Yes, bigger, at least the one I thought you'd want," Hank said, slowly understanding that Hilary and Ryan found talking about a house easier than talking about a stepmother. Maybe that was okay for now.

"Let's go," Hilary said, jumping up. "I'll get my Barbie doll. She'll want to see my new bedroom."

"Yeah, Dad," Ryan said. "Let's go. It's close, isn't it? I mean, we'll go to the same school and everything?"

"Yes, same school. Listen, kids," he said, mentally crossing his fingers, "would it be okay with you if I called Roxie and we picked her up on the way?"

"Sure, Dad," Ryan said nonchalantly. "Roxie's okay."

"Well, *Daddy*," Hilary said, pausing on the stairs up to her room and regarding him as if he were dim-witted. "Of *course* she has to go. She wants to see the house, too, if you're gonna get *married*."

Hank chuckled and shook his head. "Right, Hilary." Just like that, he thought, the discussion that he thought might take hours was over. He wouldn't be foolish enough to imagine no troubles would arise, but for now, both of his children seemed to accept the appropriateness of a new house and a new marriage. With a smile, he picked up the phone.

ROXIE COULD HARDLY WAIT for Charlie to arrive with his red rose the following morning. When he walked in, his smile a ghost of the jaunty grin he'd once had, her heart ached for him. But all would be made right today.

She hurried toward the counter as he arranged the single rose in the vase. "Hello, Charlie."

"My, but you look wonderful this morning," he said, taking off his hat and laying it on the counter.

"I should," she replied, anticipating his delight. "Hank and I are applying for a marriage license today."

Disbelief transformed itself into ecstasy on Charlie's lined face, and in his joy he did something he'd never dared before—he hurried around behind the counter into an area where, by rights, he shouldn't be. Roxie didn't say a word of protest and accepted his hug of congratulations with breathless laughter.

Ignoring the stares of her curious co-workers, she held Charlie by the shoulders and grinned at him. "Surprised you, didn't I?"

"Yes, my dear, but a more delightful surprise I've never had. How did this happen? I thought you two were at loggerheads and all was lost."

"That's the funny part. Just when I had decided that Hank was more important than having a baby, he was deciding that we should have a baby, after all."

"How delightful! Each of you willing to sacrifice for the other. Will you have the baby or not?"

"Hank insists that we'll try," Roxie said, lowering her voice as she became aware that others were listening. "But even if we can't have one, I don't mind anymore. I'll have Hank. Look, Charlie, at what he sent to the office this morning." She guided Charlie to her desk and opened a shallow box.

"Why, it's a snowflake, a giant snowflake," Charlie exclaimed, peering into the box. "How clever."

"It's white chocolate, from the shop where I bought his chocolate telephone."

"Amazing. Can you bear to eat it, or will you be like Hilary and have trouble destroying shapes?"

Roxie laughed. "Ryan and Hilary may get this. I do hate to ruin something so special."

"I suppose it signifies the day it snowed, when you first saw Hank."

"Yes, and something else, too. He sent a note with it, explaining that snowflakes are all different, of course, like people. He wanted to make sure I understood that he loves me for myself, and not as a fill-in for Sybil. Knowing that he feels that way, I don't need a baby so much."

"And because you don't need this child so much, you'll have one," Charlie predicted.

"Perhaps." Roxie smiled. "We're buying a new house, Charlie, and we'll all live there, even you. You can stay in the spare room until Hank builds a guest house."

Charlie's blue eyes twinkled, as if with a secret. "You're too kind, Roxie. I don't know what to say."

"Just say yes. The wedding's in two weeks, which will give my parents a chance to get over the shock and onto a plane. Oh, and we're taking you to lunch today, right after we settle the license business. We'll meet you at your bench and go from there."

Charlie gazed at her. "All right," he said slowly.

"Will that be a problem for you?"

"No, of course not. When will you be coming?"

"About twelve-thirty, but we might be able to change the time, if you—"

"No, Roxie," he said, laying his hand on her arm. "Twelve-thirty will be fine."

"Good. Then I'd better get back to work, before I'm fired."

"Yes." Charlie reached for her hand. "I wish you and Hank all the happiness in the world, Roxie."

Roxie squeezed his hand. "I know you do."

"I'd better be on my way, now." Charlie released his grip and returned to the other side of the counter, where he retrieved his hat. At the door he tipped it in her direction. "It's been a pleasure, my dear."

"See you at twelve-thirty," Roxie called, waving. Then she returned to her desk and forced herself to tackle the paperwork that seemed so unimportant today.

Hank arrived at noon, and by twelve twenty-five he and Roxie were walking hand in hand toward the park.

"Where shall we go for lunch?" Hank asked.

"How about El Charro? It's close by, and Charlie would

love the autographed pictures of celebrities on the walls. He might know some of them."

"Sounds good to me." He gazed down at her. "Of course everything in the past twenty-four hours has sounded good to me." He looked around as they reached the park. "Which bench is Charlie's? I don't see him."

"There." Roxie pointed to a vacant bench. "I told him twelve-thirty, and we're right on time. Where could he be?"

"I can't imagine. I thought he'd be here with bells on."

Roxie surveyed the park area, where a few people sat and ate their lunches from paper sacks, as she often had with Charlie. But the bench that had been unofficially staked out as Charlie's was empty.

Across the park, a city maintenance man stopped emptying trash cans and looked at Roxie and Hank. Then he left his job and walked toward them. "You Charlie's friends?" he asked when he was within calling distance.

"Yes." Roxie hurried forward as fear assaulted her. "Has anything happened to him?"

"Not that I know of," the man said. "But he asked me to give you this." He took a crumpled envelope from his back pocket.

Roxie took the envelope but didn't look at it. "But where is he?" she persisted.

The man shrugged. "Don't know. Said he was moving on. Probably got too hot for him here. Well, excuse me, but I have work to do." The man left.

"He can't be gone." Roxie glanced pleadingly at Hank, who was standing quietly beside her. "He wouldn't just leave, without saying goodbye, would he?"

"I don't know, Roxie," Hank said, touching her shoulder. "Maybe you'd better open the envelope."

With trembling fingers Roxie tore open the envelope and

almost dropped the figure-eight gold pin that fell out of it. "Oh, Charlie," she murmured, holding the pin. "You did say that you gave the pin away at the end."

"At the end of what?" Hank asked.

"At the end of each job as St. Valentine. But it doesn't matter. There's an endless supply of pins."

"Roxie, are you saying that you think he's really—"

She gazed up at Hank. "I don't know. I just don't know anymore."

"What else is in the envelope?"

"A letter." She unfolded the paper. "This is very good-quality stationery. Where would he get such good stationery?"

Hank shook his head. "Wherever he gets the gold pins, I guess."

"And look at this gold embossing on the top. The letter 'A' with a crown on top, and an inscription underneath. Can you read Latin?"

"No." Hank studied the embossed words. "But maybe I can figure it out. *Amor* means *love* and *vincit* probably is like *invincible*."

"Of course," Roxie said. "And the last word, *omnia*, means *all*. Love Conquers All. It's a common phrase. He used it himself once."

"You realize that Charlie could have had that made up in any print shop in Tucson."

"I suppose."

"But you don't think he did, do you?"

"I really don't know what to think. Let's read what he said."

Together they scanned the brief note.

Dear Ones,
My work here is finished and I must prepare for my

next adventure in love. I leave you knowing that your future together is bright, for you have been blessed by the special magic of St. Valentine's Day. For a brief while I feared that the spell no longer worked, but now my faith is restored and I must continue my journey. Give my love to Como and tell the Osborns that she prefers Shakespeare to Kipling.

My fondest regards,
St. Valentine (Charlie Hartman)

Slowly Roxie folded the letter and tucked it back in the envelope. "I don't know what to believe," she said, gazing up at Hank.

"I do." His gray eyes were warm with affection. "I believe that Charlie Hartman, whoever he is, gave me the chance to love a wonderful woman, and thank God I didn't blow the chance. Whether Charlie is really St. Valentine doesn't matter anymore. Our love is real, and that's all that counts."

"I will miss him, Hank."

"So will I." He put his arm around her and led her away from the park. "But we have a lifetime to comfort each other, my beloved."

_____ Epilogue _____

THE DRIVER of the eighteen-wheeler was talkative, so Charlie obliged him with conversation to while away the hours.

"Must be nice," the driver said, "to pick up and go whenever you want. Tucson gets too hot, you head for the mountains to wait out the summer. Nobody has you on a schedule. Not a bad life, old man."

"No, it isn't a bad life," Charlie agreed. "But you're mistaken about the schedule. I do have one. By September I have to settle down somewhere and make preparations."

The driver looked puzzled. "Preparations?"

"Yes, and they must be carefully handled. I have to create a base of operations, locate and find suitable people."

"What you got, some sort of con game going on?"

"Heavens no, young man. My purposes are purely philanthropic."

"If you say so."

"But everything must proceed on schedule, just as you are required to deliver your merchandise on time. I can't afford to miss my all-important deadline."

"What deadline?"

"Why February fourteenth, of course, young man. It's the most important day of the year for lovers." Charlie leaned back against the seat and smiled. "Still."

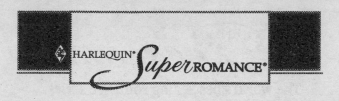

HARLEQUIN®
INTRIGUE

WE'LL LEAVE YOU BREATHLESS!

If you've been looking for thrilling tales of contemporary passion and sensuous love stories with taut, edge-of-the-seat suspense—then you'll love Harlequin Intrigue!

Every month, you'll meet four new heroes who are guaranteed to make your spine tingle and your pulse pound. With them you'll enter into the exciting world of Harlequin Intrigue— where your life is on the line and so is your heart!

THAT'S INTRIGUE—
ROMANTIC SUSPENSE
AT ITS BEST!

HARLEQUIN®
Makes any time special ®

Harlequin® Historical

From rugged lawmen and valiant knights to defiant heiresses and spirited frontierswomen, Harlequin Historicals will capture your imagination with their dramatic scope, passion and adventure.

Harlequin Historicals... they're too good to miss!

HHDIR1

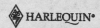